ABOUT THE AU

GEORGE G. GILMAN was born in 1936 in what was then a small village east of London. He attended local schools until the age of fifteen. Upon leaving school he abandoned all earlier ambitions and decided to become a professional writer, with strong leanings towards the mystery novel. Wrote short stories and books during evenings, lunch hours, at weekends, and on the time of various employers while he worked for an international newsagency, a film company, a weekly book-trade magazine and the Royal Air Force.

His first short (love) story was published when he was sixteen and the first (mystery) novel ten years later. He has been a full-time writer since 1970, writing mostly Westerns which have been translated into a dozen languages and have sold in excess of 15 million copies. He is married with a dog and lives on the Dorset coast, which is as far west as he intends to move right now.

The STEELE series by George G. Gilman published by New English Library

ADAM STEELE 1: THE VIOLENT PEACE
ADAM STEELE 2: BOUNTY HUNTER
ADAM STEELE 3: HELL'S JUNCTION
ADAM STEELE 4: VALLEY OF BLOOD
ADAM STEELE 5: GUN RUN
ADAM STEELE 6: THE KILLING ART
ADAM STEELE 7: CROSS-FIRE
ADAM STEELE 8: COMANCHE CARNAGE
ADAM STEELE 9: BADGE IN THE DUST
ADAM STEELE 10: THE LOSERS
ADAM STEELE 11: LYNCH TOWN
ADAM STEELE 12: DEATH TRAIL
ADAM STEELE 13: BLOODY BORDER
ADAM STEELE 14: DELTA DUEL
ADAM STEELE 15: RIVER OF DEATH
ADAM STEELE 16: NIGHTMARE AT NOON
ADAM STEELE 17: SATAN'S DAUGHTERS
ADAM STEELE 18: THE HARD WAY
ADAM STEELE 19: THE TARNISHED STAR
ADAM STEELE 20: WANTED FOR MURDER
ADAM STEELE 21: WAGONS EAST
ADAM STEELE 22: THE BIG GAME
ADAM STEELE 23: FORT DESPAIR
ADAM STEELE 24: MANHUNT
ADAM STEELE 25: STEELE'S WAR: THE WOMAN
ADAM STEELE 26: STEELE'S WAR: THE PREACHER
ADAM STEELE 27: STEELE'S WAR: THE STOREKEEPER
ADAM STEELE 28: STEELE'S WAR: THE STRANGER
ADAM STEELE 29: THE BIG PRIZE
ADAM STEELE 30: THE KILLER MOUNTAINS
ADAM STEELE 31: THE CHEATERS
ADAM STEELE 32: THE WRONG MAN
ADAM STEELE 33: THE VALLEY OF THE SHADOW
ADAM STEELE 34: THE RUNAWAY
ADAM STEELE 35: STRANGER IN A STRANGE TOWN
ADAM STEELE 36: THE HELLRAISERS
ADAM STEELE 37: CANYON OF DEATH

EDGE MEETS ADAM STEELE: TWO OF A KIND
EDGE MEETS ADAM STEELE: MATCHING PAIR
EDGE MEETS ADAM STEELE: DOUBLE ACTION

CANYON OF DEATH

George G. Gilman

NEW ENGLISH LIBRARY

A New English Library Original Publication, 1985

First NEL Paperback Edition March 1985

NEL Books are published by
New English Library,
Mill Road, Dunton Green,
Sevenoaks, Kent.
Editorial office: 47 Bedford Square, London WC1B 3DP

Typeset by Hewer Text Composition Services, Edinburgh

Made and printed in Great Britain by Hunt Barnard, Aylesbury, Bucks.

British Library Cataloguing in Publication Data
Gilman, George G.
Canyon of death.—(Adam Steele; no. 37)
Rn: Terry Harknett I. Title II. Series
823'.914[F] PR6058.A686

ISBN: 0 450 05810 7

for:
Greville Beach
from way back down
a lot of trails

ONE

IT WAS early morning when Adam Steele, Amos Quinn and Mary-Ann Slattery broke their night camp and headed toward the canyon: the Virginian astride his black stallion while the old man and the widow woman rode on the seat of the heavily-laden farm wagon, Quinn in control of the pair of geldings in the traces. The leading curve of the new day's sun was showing above the rugged horizon formed by the Chuska Mountains, but as yet it provided just soft light and pleasing warmth. Soon, the cloudless blue of the Arizona sky promised, the same sun would start to deliver hour upon hour of harsh brightness and broiling heat.

'It's gonna be another hot one and no mistake about that,' Quinn growled with a querulous glance across the expanse of parched scrub desert toward the distant mountain ridges. 'Hotter than yesterday, I reckon.'

'It'll feel like it is sure enough, Mr Quinn,' the woman responded absently as she gazed directly ahead, over the backs of the team horses and past the rider who was leading them along the well-trodden trail that went into the canyon at the very centre of its mile-wide mouth.

'Spring almost done and summer all but here, it'll more than just feel like it, Mrs Slattery,' the old man countered.

'I'm sure you're right,' she agreed in a tone and with a sigh that drew Quinn's attention to her. And, as he saw her expression in profile, his attitude altered from peevishness to apology. But he did not voice his feelings – merely reached to the side and rested a gnarled hand in the crook of her elbow. She responded by turning briefly to look at him, with an expression that came close to being a smile. But there were tears latent in her eyes and her lower lip trembled when she made to alter the line of her mouth. He nodded and she touched his hand with her fingertips. Then, as the physical contact was broken, she assured: 'It's all right, Mr Quinn.' She swallowed hard but decided against a second attempt at a smile as she resumed her watch on the terrain ahead. 'No tears this morning. I don't need talk to keep from bawling, either.'

'Whatever you say, Mrs Slattery,' he allowed pensively.

'But if you want to talk,' she hurried to tell him. 'If it helps you to . . .'

'Grand-daughters ain't like husbands,' the old man said into the pause after she had failed to find a way to finish what she had started, her mind having again drifted away from the here and now to what once had been. 'Truth to tell, I been over it several days now . . . the urge to break down any time and any place part of it, I mean. Never will get over losin' Jane entirely. Just like I never have gotten over losin' her Ma and my own dear wife that bore Jane's Ma and . . . hell, a man don't get to be my age without seein' a whole bunch of folks he loves get put in the ground. And, since you got one part of your grief beat, I ain't nothin' but a mule-brained old man for rekindling morbid ashes.'

'I'm much obliged for all the support you've given me, Mr Quinn,' she told him as the creaking wagon rolled over the unmarked line between the open desert and the canyon bottom at its broad mouth. And there was a fleeting smile of gratitude on her face as Steele glanced back at her while the old man countered:

'We've been good for each other, my dear. And nothin' is owed to anyone. Ain't that right, young feller?'

His tone became as light as that of the woman as he raised his voice to pose the query to the Virginian who was facing front again.

'Was never stated, old man, but right from the outset we've been three different people who just happen to be heading in the same direction at the same time.'

'Oh, it's never been quite so clear-cut as that, Mr Steele,' the woman said quickly. 'We aren't strangers to each other who happen to be travelling the same road.'

The Virginian, who spoke with an accent that suggested he had only recently left his native state, this time made no response to the implied question. And, while his back remained firmly toward the couple riding the wagon, the man with the reins and the woman at his side exchanged wistful glances that tacitly expressed more than a thousand words could have done about their mutual understanding of the mood of the rider leading them into the canyon.

The garb of Adam Steele would further have misled a stranger into gaining a first impression that he was a newcomer to the primitive south-west: for he wore an Eastern style blue-black suit, of expensive cloth and cut, over an elegant cream-coloured vest and white shirt; a scarf tied loosely in cravat fashion at his throat. His hat was a grey Stetson with a black band of tooled leather. Black was also the colour of his riding boots and the tight-fitting buckskin gloves.

The man so dudishly attired was not tall nor broad. Not young, either, but not so old as he looked. He was just a shade over five and a half feet and his frame was built on lean lines: with very little fat and the kind of muscular strength that came far short of being bulgingly obvious. His face was comprised of the kind of features that became more attractive as he aged, and harsh times and the ravages of the elements took their toll. His eyes were coal black, his mouthline was gentle and his skin was dark brown and heavily scored. His short-cut hair no longer showed any trace of its former redness, its all over grey tending to make him look more than a year or two over his true, early forties age: except when he infrequently showed a smile that was still somehow boyish.

It was a long time since he rode away from Virginia in the wake of the War Between the States, and since then the closest he had ever got to the land of his birth and upbringing was New Orleans. Once again, though, he was seeking for a place to put down roots and call home, in the no-longer alien country of the west. And, as he set an easy pace along the floor of the narrowing canyon in the rising heat of developing morning, he was host to expanding doubt about his impulsive decision to tie up with the couple riding aboard the wagon in back of him.

Amos Quinn was about seventy years old. Tall and thin, grey-haired and with hardly a tooth in his head. He had deep-set, dark-coloured eyes and wrinkled skin that hung loosely on a bone structure that in years gone by had been more thickly fleshed out.

The woman who sat beside him was half his age. Tall for one of her sex with a fine, slender build. She was attractive without being beautiful. A natural blonde, she had a fair skin with freckles scattered lightly across her cheeks beneath her blue, almond-shaped eyes. Her lips were thin above a chin with a shallow cleft cut into it.

Quinn, who owned the wagon on which they rode and most of the freight loaded aboard it, wore brown dungarees, a frayed shirt of indeterminate colour and a hat and boots which had outlived their useful lives. He did not wear any sign of being in mourning. While Mary-Ann Slattery's broad-brimmed white hat and modestly loose-fitting white dress, despite being subdued by the trail dust of many miles, served to emphasize by contrast the jet-black band that encircled her left upper arm. Just a few of the household chattels and a tin trunk of clothes on the wagon belonged to her.

Adam Steele, who never grieved for the dead any more, and seldom felt regret about anything, carried all his possessions on his back or the horse he rode.

Strangers to each other these three most certainly were not. The tragic gunning down of Jane Quinn and the wanton killing of Neil Slattery had thrown them together in the west Texas town of Barclay something over four weeks ago. The single-street community could have been just one more peaceful stopover on the long trail the Virginian was riding, from what the war had left him with toward whatever compromise it was his ultimate decision to accept. But it happened that in Barclay he was destined to once more become involved in an eruption of violence which drew him yet again into kill or be killed situations. Usually, he was able to ride away from such close calls with death in the same manner he left those towns where he stopped off to rest up, buy supplies or get his horse re-shod: quickly forgetting their names, the names of the people he had become involved with, and even the nature of the violence into which he was drawn.

But, as he was bedding down for the night when he was two days of easy riding away from Barclay, the heavily-laden wagon with its driver and one passenger had rolled to a halt on the fringe of the glow from his dying fire. Inevitably, events of the recent past rather than any unwritten code had urged the Virginian into sharing his camp with the ill-matched couple who had decided individually that Barclay no longer held anything for them and acted in concert to leave the place. Then, in the morning, with just the one trail to follow and nobody in greater haste than anybody else to travel it, it would have been less than natural for the rider and the man and woman aboard the wagon not to move out together.

'Anytime you wanna move off the trail with that mount of yours,' Quinn said suddenly to end a lengthy period of vocal silence. 'Or you take it into your head to make more speed than we can with his rig, you just go ahead and do it.'

'I don't have to say thanks for that, feller,' Steele told the old-timer, and glanced at him and the woman beside him as part of a glance over his shoulder that took in the wagon, the team and the terrain back to the canyon mouth and beyond. And he saw Quinn scowl and Mary-Ann sigh before he swept his gaze to the flanking rims of the hundred-feet-high sandstone walls, next the boulder- and brush-scattered areas at the bases of the cliffs. Then directed his cold-eyed attention to where the trail crested an almost undiscernible rise, before dropping out of sight where the canyon narrowed to maybe fifty feet in width a half mile or so ahead.

'It was never stated, either,' the woman said in a melancholy tone as the Virginian continued his cautious surveillance over their surroundings – something she had been aware of him doing to a greater or lesser extent from almost the first moment she met him. 'But none of us have any strings attached to the other.'

'Though why it should be this mornin' you decide you don't want no more truck with us, young feller, I just can't understand,' Quinn complained with a pensive shake of his head.

'He's getting around to putting it into words now, Mr Quinn,' Mary-Ann explained as she peered expectantly at Steele's back, waiting for a denial. 'I think he's been having second thoughts about us for a long time. Perhaps from the very first day.'

'Still don't answer what I brought up,' the old-timer insisted fractiously. 'Seems to me ain't neither you nor me done anythin' out of the way to get his back up?'

Steele could sense both of them gazing at him now, willing him to respond to the implied question. And it irritated him, for as he became conscious of their guileless interest in him he had begun to be aware of the possibility that all three of them were being secretly and perhaps menacingly watched. But whatever signal his sixth sense for imminent danger had picked up out of the oven-heated air of the canyon floor, it was abruptly negated by the near-palpable tacit pressure directed at him by his travelling companions.

'Could be,' the Virginian started in the rasping tone of anger controlled by a short leash, then forced moderation into his voice to complete: 'that all the talking you people do without saying anything has finally reached a raw nerve? You think that could be it?'

He made another cold-eyed survey of their surroundings as he gave the reply, but saw no sign of a covert watcher in the area of the narrowing canyon which provided the ideal situation for an ambush. While the rims of the towering walls remained totally inanimate against the glaring brightness of the sky and the horizon beyond the distant mouth of the canyon showed only the illusion of movement with mirages in the shimmering heat haze. And he decided, as he glimpsed the old-timer and the widow woman as parts of the entire scene, that the sensation of being threatened by an unseen enemy had been an illusion: created out of recognizing just how perfect a place this was for an ambuscade, while part of his mind was concerned with the kind of trap in which he was already ensnared.

'Hell, young feller, you said it yourself . . . not that I needed to be told. The worst kinda grief there is, is lonesome grief. And sometimes the only kinda help that does any good is talk. About anythin' under the sun. Didn't you say that? Didn't he say that, Mrs Slattery?'

Amos Quinn had begun to snarl the defensive retort, but finished up with a pleading tone of self-doubt.

'And meant it when he said it, I am certain,' the woman answered as she laid a reassuring hand on the old-timer's forearm. 'But it's taken a long time and a great deal of perhaps empty talk to heal the hurt thus far. And for a man such as Adam Steele, who I would hazard is never entirely at ease in the company of . . .'

She was peering fixedly at the suit-jacketed back of the Virginian again, and was tense in expectation of a perhaps angry interruption. But it was the abrupt manner in which Steele reined his horse to a halt that caused her to curtail what she was suggesting. A moment before he told her:

'Never have been a company man, Mrs Slattery. But I reckon you could say that for the last couple of days I've been a member of the bored.'

He had brought his stallion to a stop a few feet short of the crest of the gently-rising canyon floor: in a position that gave him a clear view down a shorter and steeper incline toward a stone and timber building with a corral and a stable at the rear to the west side of the trail. A quarter mile distant.

'It's gratifying to know that our grief hasn't robbed you of your sense of humour,' the woman said with just a hint of relief: as if she had been concerned about angering Steele further by revealing how well she understood some aspects of his character.

Then, as the old-timer rolled the wagon to a halt so that the seat was level with where the rider sat his horse, and she and Quinn were able to look down on the same scene as Steele, Mary-Ann Slattery felt her anxiety allayed still further: and viewed what was apparently a stage-line way station with smiling eyes. And the old man began to express a similar degree of quiet pleasure at the prospect of seeing some fresh faces: until he ended his blurred survey of the distant way station and was able to focus more clearly on the grim set profile of Steele just a few feet to his left. When he asked doubtfully:

'You see somethin' these old eyes of mine missed, young feller?'

The woman heard the uneasiness in the voice of Amos Quinn and glanced at the old-timer and the Virginian for a second or so. Her near delight faded and she gazed fearfully down at the peaceful scene below for as long as it took Steele to answer in an even tone that was an ill-match for his expression:

'Nothing that says there's trouble waiting for us down there, Mr Quinn. But nothing that says there isn't, either.'

'Good grief. you look for evil behind every stick and stone we come across!' the woman exclaimed impatiently when she completed her careful study of the quiet buildings of the way station and the horses which were almost motionless in the mid-morning heat – four of them with saddles on their backs, standing in the full glare of the sun at the hitching rail out front of the main building, and six others bare-backed in a patch of shade in the corral at the rear. 'I think we should move —'

A violent fusillade of gunshots exploded in the main building. Maybe six or seven. A man screamed his agony – or perhaps his terror of dying. Another vented an obscenity. And a third laughed in demonic enjoyment of the carnage. As black powder-smoke began to drift lethargically out through the open doorway, and the saddle-horses hitched to the rail backed off from its acrid stench to the limit of their reins, Amos Quinn gulped and hissed:

'Shit.'

Steele murmured in a grim tone that was now compatible with his expression: 'That mean the motion's been passed?'

TWO

ALL SOUND from within the building below was ended as abruptly as it had begun. The horses at the front moved forward again to take the tautness out of their reins as soon as the gunsmoke and its taint had been negated by the outside air. The most skittish of the animals in the corral scraped at the arid, hard-packed ground for a few more moments, but then became as calm as the others in the wake of the violence.

'How on earth could you have known?' Mary-Ann Slattery murmured, her voice a harsh but hardly audible whisper as she and Quinn found their gazes trapped to the open doorway – beyond which the silence seemed more intense now that death had paid a visit there.

The old-timer had to swallow hard again before he could trust himself to speak. 'He didn't, is my opinion,' he answered as Steele raked his unblinking gaze around every point of the compass. 'It's like you said, Mrs Slattery. He expects it behind every . . .'

He interrupted his own growled response as the woman laid a frightened hand on his arm: both of them reacting to a stirring of activity below. And the Virginian, having seen no movement of any kind elsewhere, directed his attention to what was happening at the foot of the slope beyond the narrowest point of the canyon. Was in time to see three men emerge backwards across the threshold of the way-station doorway.

The first one to backstep into sight carried a rifle sloped nonchalantly to his shoulder, and he remained at his full height as he came to a halt with a hip against the hitching rail, where it ended at an upright opposite a jamb of the unporched doorway. Where he watched, and perhaps issued instructions to the other two as they emerged into the glare of the hot sun. Each of these carried a rifle, too, but held low down as they reversed out of the building in awkward half-crouches, free hands clasped to the wrists of corpses.

'I am awake?' Mary-Ann Slattery gasped. 'This isn't a nightmare?'

'You're awake, lady,' Quinn answered sourly. But then became consoling as he touched her arm briefly and reminded: 'This is nothin' to do with us, my dear. We can't mourn for strangers.'

The dead were a man and a woman, each with blood in their hair and staining their clothes. A great deal of blood – enough so that twin trails of quick-to-darken crimson were left on the parched ground as the corpses were unceremoniously dragged across the front of the building and across a vegetable plot at the far side, from where the trio on the crest of the rise watched.

'Weren't young, I'd say,' Amos Quinn murmured. 'Way they was white-haired.'

'Does that make it any better?' the woman countered bitterly.

'Just talkin'. Sorry. And for cussin' the way I done when the shootin' got started.'

'And I apologize for misunderstanding your meaning, Mr Quinn,' she answered softly.

'Please call me old man, my dear,' the old-timer urged, and she nodded and accepted the offer of his open palm. Then, as they drew mutual comfort from their joined hands, they glanced at Steele before resuming their horrified watch on the disposal of the bodies. And, as they saw the utter dispassion with which the Virginian looked down upon the same scene, each of them spontaneously held more tightly to the hand of the other – as if in tacit agreement to disassociate themselves from Steele in his present state of mind.

There was a well on the far side of the vegetable patch, and it was to this that the blood-dripping, bullet-shattered corpses were dragged: neat rows of carefully-tended lettuce and cabbage and carrot and onion getting trampled and knocked down by the killers and their victims.

When they reached the well, each of the men leaned his rifle against the surrounding wall, and the one who had obviously the top hand cranked the handle to bring a pail of water to the surface.

There was a dipper in the bucket and all three took a drink. Then, as brutally oblivious as they had been before to dignity in death, all three contributed to the chore of lifting the corpses up off the ground and tipping them head first down the well.

Mary-Ann Slattery shuddered twice – each time the far-off sound of a water splash reached up to the top of the slope. Or perhaps she only imagined she heard the limply-falling bodies impact with the underground water. For certainly, as they picked up their rifles and ambled back toward and into the way station, not a word of what the men said to each other carried to within earshot of the watchers.

'Do you think the man who killed Neil was as callous as . . . ?' the woman began tautly.

'Hush, my dear,' Quinn told her and eased his hand gently out of her grip so that he could take up the reins of the two horse team in the traces. 'Like I said, what we just seen ain't no concern of ours. What we gotta concern ourselves with is the two choices we gotta decide between.'

At last able to wrench her gaze away from the once more serenely peaceful-looking way station, Mary-Ann Slattery discovered that the old-timer was aping the actions of Adam Steele in the way he scanned every sunlit and shadowed area on all sides of them – and above on the canyon rims.

'Choices?' she whispered.

'Roll on down and by that place and hope them killers inside figure it's best for their interests to let us go through. Or turn around and head back the way we just come. And then make another decision. Whether to find another trail to follow someplace or to wait until them fellers below get through with what they're here for and take off.'

'Since they failed to spot us, Mr Quinn,' the woman said, forgetting her promise to address him the way he liked, 'I think it would be foolhardy to try to pass immediately. For they must surely realize we would have heard the gunshots?'

'That's good thinkin', Mrs Slattery,' Quinn growled, content to retain the formality in their relationship during the present tense situation.

'Also, in country such as this is, travellers would hardly pass by an obviously occupied house without stopping to pass the time of day.'

'To at least ask if they could refill their canteens and water barrel from a sweet water well, Mrs Slattery,' Quinn added.

'This is all empty talk again,' the woman said, concern giving way to puzzlement as both men interrupted their all-around surveillance: Steele to peer thoughtfully down at the way station, while Quinn eyed the younger man inquiringly. 'So why don't we start to withdraw right now?'

'Four horses are hitched to the rail outside the place down there and just three men been seen, Mrs Slattery,' the old-timer pointed out. 'Question is, did the one that ain't been seen get shot inside the place or is he out here somewhere on watch?'

Now the woman began to peer at her surroundings, uneasily conscious of the countless places where a secret watcher could be in hiding. And then pointed out: 'If he was shot in the fighting, surely they'd have put him down the well with the other two?'

'If he wasn't shot dead, he'd most likely have objected to that, Mrs Slattery,' Steele answered.

'And I reckon from the — ' Quinn began.

But the woman interrupted eagerly: 'Or it could be a spare horse, couldn't it? It's a stage depot down there. Perhaps those three men are waiting to meet somebody from off the next stage and the horse — '

'No, I don't think that can be so,' the old-timer said dejectedly. And arched his eyebrows to make it a query addressed to Steele as the woman's newly found enthusiasm faded as fast as it had been created.

'You were going to say before the lady thought of that, feller?' the Virginian asked.

Quinn's gaunt and heavily-lined face showed resignation in the wake of dejection and he vented a sigh before he answered: 'Damnit, young feller, I reckon you're as sure as I am we've got ourselves into some kinda trap. And that the sonsofbitches – beg your pardon, ma'am – that got us caught are either toyin' with us or waitin' for a better chance to spring it.'

The woman's fear expanded as she listened to the embittered voice of Quinn while she constantly switched her gaze between his dejected face and the impassive features of Adam Steele. But then she was able to keep a check on her uneasiness by indulging in acid anger. 'Is all this to show me how empty talk can get on a person's nerves, Mr Steele?' she demanded. 'I can assure you it's working if that is what — '

'We all saw the same thing, lady,' Steele pointed out. 'It should occur to you that so did the three men down at the way station.'

'Of course they did! They did the killing and — '

'All three of them saw all three of us, Mrs Slattery,' Quinn cut across what she was saying and caused her rising anger to be curtailed by fresh dread, as she wrenched her head around to stare again down at the serene scene at the foot of the slope a quarter mile or so away.

'But not one of them so much as cast a glance in this direction while — '

'They didn't look at anything except what they were doing,' Steele reminded her.

'More you think about that, more it seems not a natural thing to do, ma'am,' the old timer added. 'Us sittin' up here large as life, without no time to back off outta sight after the shootin' got started. And them three fellers just drag the dead outta the depot, dump the carcases in the well and go on back inside. Without — '

'You're right!' Mary-Ann said with a gulp. 'I was so stunned by the brutal way they . . . they were just too obvious in seeming not to know we were up here watching them?'

'Saw us from inside the place. Maybe even before they killed that old couple. And it didn't take them long to decide to brazen it out. Dump the carcases like they was gettin' rid of the house garbage.'

'To try to frighten us away?' the woman suggested with scant conviction. And switched her gaze fast between Steele and Quinn and the way station.

'Scare us into somethin', and no mistake,' the old-timer said. 'And I reckon we've near enough run outta talk about what it done, uh young feller?'

'Looks like the fellers down there have run out of something, too,' the Virginian murmured. And moved his right hand away from where it had been draped over his saddlehorn with the left that loosely held the reins: let it rest on his thigh close to where the fire-scorched rosewood stock of a Colt Hartford revolving rifle jutted from the forward-hung boot.

There was slight movement visible beyond the sunlit doorway of the way station and Mary-Ann Slattery caught her breath and reached out once more to grasp Amos Quinn's hand when she realized the trio of killers were about to emerge from the building.

'Patience, you reckon?' the old-timer said in a croaking tone as the top man led the other two across the threshold: all with their rifles canted to shoulders now as they gazed fixedly out from the shadows of their hat-brims up to where he and the widow sat aboard the stalled wagon, and the Virginian remained astride the stallion.

'Or time,' Steele said. And began to ease his hand closer to the booted rifle as he turned his head and the three men came to a halt in a ragged line behind the horses hitched to the rail out front of the way station.

But the Apache was already poised to kill the woman. In the time it took to squeeze the trigger of his aimed Winchester. While the gloved hand of the Virginian was still more than an inch away from making contact with his own rifle.

'You try, she die,' the young, good-looking, athletically-built Indian brave warned, as he rose to his full height of nearly six feet on the nearside of the wagon; the muzzle of the repeater aimed from his shoulder held at an unwavering distance of three feet from the downslope of Mary-Ann's left breast.

'Oh my God, no – Indians!' the woman gasped as she snapped her head around and expressed depthless terror as she pushed herself hard against the back of the seat, her fingers becoming like talons that dug into the back of Quinn's hand.

'Just the one, I reckon?' Steele said, and posed it as a query to the brave who was dressed in the same Western-style garb as the trio at the way station, except that instead of a Stetson he wore a decorated headband with an eagle's feather at the back.

'Where the hell did he spring from?' the old-timer croaked.

'Just the one, but one of the best, I think you must agree,' the Apache said, and remained tensed to respond to the first sign of aggression, as he displayed a smile of pride in the achievement of getting as close to the whites as he needed before his presence was detected.

'Hey, Charlie!'

The woman and the old-timer glanced down toward the men out front of the way station, and saw that the one in command had cupped his free hand to his mouth to amplify the harsh sound of his voice. This as Steele kept his attention riveted on the Apache, whose smile became one of invitation to recklessness and confidence in his ability to stay in control of whatever situation was set to develop.

'You, dude, and you, old man. You'll use your hands only for the reins.' The well-spoken instructions by the brave recaptured the attention of Quinn and Mary-Ann. 'And you, pretty lady, will be the first to meet your maker if either of them gives me the slightest cause. Now, move on down the hill. The same easy speed you came this far. And with the dude out front as before. Do that now.'

Just for part of a second, when Steele returned both his hands to the reins and heeled his stallion into movement, the Apache flicked his dark eyes along their narrowed sockets to peer with a trace of concern back along the canyon floor toward its northern end and the heat-shimmered scrub desert beyond. And, as he moved out in front of the wagon which Quinn began to roll in his wake, Steele directed a brief glance back over his own shoulder. But saw nothing except sun-baked dirt, red rock, parched vegetation, blue sky and the slick-looking heat haze. Was disconsertingly aware, though, that this was all he had seen many times over, while this arrogant young Apache who obviously retained his native cunning behind the facade of an educated white man had remained hidden, and perhaps moving, in the glaringly brightly-lit landscape.

Then, as he turned to face the way he was going again, the Virginian found his attention fleetingly held by something hung from the gunbelt of the Indian, who continued to keep his rifle fixedly aimed at the increasingly nervous Mary-Ann, while he strolled easily along beside the slow-rolling wagon: a brass telescope.

'What's this all about, young feller?' Quinn squeezed from his throat that was constricted by the same brand of fear as that which held the woman in the petrified attitude pressed to the back of the seat. But it was apparent from the way he stared ahead, past Steele on the stallion, that it was the trio of white men rather than the Apache brave who caused his stomach to churn, hands to twitch and cheek to spasm.

'Let me ask you something, old man?'

'Sure. Anythin', young feller.'

'Since Merle Thorne and Doc Harding and Luther Schuler and me, Charlie Smiles, have got you people well and truly covered . . . you understand?'

'Yeah.' Quinn nodded vigorously.

'Why the frig should any of us tell you a frigging thing, old man?'

Amos Quinn experienced a stab of anger, but vented just a muted groan of frustration when the woman at his side sensed the danger and deliberately dug the nails of her claw-like fingers into his hand.

'Hell, Charlie!' one of the three men out front of the way station called, as all of them brought their rifles to the aim when the distance from the top of the incline had been halved, 'couldn't you have taken care of them out along the trail? Instead of lettin' them get this close to clutter the place up?'

'Make less with the mouth, Luther,' the leader of the bunch growled, and ignored the three strangers to gaze at the Apache when he went on: 'You ever known Charlie to do anything without there was good reason?'

Luther Schuler glowered his dislike of the Apache, but injected some false contrition into his tone when he responded: 'I guess not, Merle.'

The man who was, by process of elimination, Doc Harding, said with a leer and a tone of lustful relish: 'The woman'll maybe help to fill the time while we're waitin' for the stage, Merle?'

A gesture of Thorne's rifle and a movement of his head caused Steele to rein in his mount and Quinn to bring the wagon to a halt. A few feet from where the three Winchester-toting white men stood in the uneven line – one leering, one scowling and the other coldly impassive.

Then Mary-Ann shivered and gasped as she tried to press herself even harder against the back of the seat: like she felt there was something tangible in the lascivious stare of Harding that she sensed reaching out to touch her body. But this flinching from the drooling look of the lecherous man was not enough to ease the gnawing horror in her mind.

And so, driven by a terror close to hysteria, she sprang to her feet, whirled, and screamed shrilly as she hurled herself off the wagon at the Apache: 'I'll die first!'

Merle Thorne emphasized his readiness to blast a bullet into Steele – thrust the muzzle of his rifle six inches closer to the target of the Virginian's chest, left of centre.

Steele, who had his head half-turned to watch what was happening at the wagon, remained unmoving except for his lips to form the words as he growled: 'That's a race I'm not entered for.'

THREE

HAD AMOS QUINN been a younger and fitter man, he would probably have died a second or so after the woman lunged into her clawed-handed attack on the Apache. But, although his instincts to go to the aid of Mary-Ann were instantaneous with the start of her move to throw herself off the side of the wagon, his physical reflexes had suffered too much from the ravages of time to comply fast enough with what he demanded of them.

Thus, as the Virginian turned in his saddle and made it plain to the three white men with rifles that he had no intention of interfering in the woman's reckless action, it was seen to be equally obvious that the old-timer was unable to take a hand – as he tried to rise and twist to the side and dive through the same falling arc as Mary-Ann. For, with a grimace of pain displacing the frown of dread on his thin face, he was able only to get part way to his feet and make a part turn before the sudden strain this placed upon time- and tension-stiffened muscles pulled him heavily back down on to the seat again. And Merle Thorne growled out of the side of his mouth:

'Let it go boys!'

The rifles of Schuler and Harding continued to be negligently aimed at the old man, who sat immobile on the wagon seat, with tears that were doubtless of frustration rather than pain glistening in the corners of his dark eyes.

Thorne paid more attention to the way in which he kept the Virginian covered, but was so positioned that he was able to do this and also watch how Charlie Smiles dealt with the enraged and terrified woman. The Apache achieving this in little more time than it took for Steele and Thorne to voice their comments and Quinn to submit to the inevitability of old age.

His good-looking face split by a broad grin of limitless self-confidence again, the Indian stepped to the side and swung into a half turn. His moves fluid and graceful so that the impulsive actions of the woman he appeared to be retreating from seemed even more clumsy by contrast. She tried to turn in mid-air, flailing her arms in a doomed effort to clutch at the brave's rifle barrel with one hand while the other scratched viciously at the pleasure-wreathed face. Her shriek of anger and fear became a wail of distress as she realized she had failed. Then the shrillness was gone from her tone, and she vented a low pitched cry of pain when her right shoulder and hip took the agonizing brunt of her impact with the rock-hard ground.

The violence of the sudden end to the plunge knocked the breath out of her, and the sound coming from her gaping mouth was reduced to a choked gasping as she remained on her right side with her sucked-in belly a few inches away from the Apache's feet. Her unmoving head rested on the wrist of her right arm, while her left arm was draped on the ground behind her, in an attitude that emphasized the unspectacular but attractive swells of her rapidly rising and falling breasts within the contours of her dress bodice.

That was all it had taken to subdue the woman; but now, as if he resented the ease of the victory and his pride demanded positive action in case his agile move away from the woman be misconstrued by the watchers, the Apache kicked his right foot lightly forward. With just sufficient force to land the toe of his boot against Mary-Ann's left hip and tip her over on to her back, rather than with any object of causing her pain. And now, with one arm trapped under her back, the other sprawled out to the side the woman, who still had to struggle for breath, uttered a groan that was of humiliation rather than fear, as she felt the pressure of the brave's rifle muzzle nudge against her body. As with the kick that had rolled her on to her back, the Apache did not seek to inflict pain with the Winchester – rested it on rather than made any attempt to push it through the fabric of the white dress and into the intimacy of Mary-Ann's flesh at the crotch.

She lay immobile except for her laboured breathing, and silent but for the rasping of the hot air into and out of her constricted throat. From when she started her vain attempt to get herself killed until she hit the ground and knew she was helpless, perhaps not two full seconds had elapsed. Then, in the tense silence that she alone kept from being absolute, and in which she endured pain because of her own actions and degradation at the whim of the Apache while he relished setting the seal on his victory, more than ten seconds slid into the past.

'Hey, that ain't necessary, Charlie,' Harding rasped between teeth gritted in a fixed smile, while his lust-filled eyes drank in the obscene sight of the rifle barrel pressed to Mary-Ann's body. 'I ain't never come across one yet that didn't already have right there a — '

'Don't make me out to be a liar, Charlie,' Thorne cut softly in on what the other man was saying.

'Boss?' the Apache posed, still holding the humiliated gaze of the woman's eyes in the trap of his smiling ones.

'Merle claims you don't ever do a friggin' thing unless there's good reason, Injun!' Schuler growled, his tone and the expression on his face emphatically confirming his hostile antipathy toward the brave. 'You didn't send these horses' asses to the white eyes' happy huntin' ground already, like I said once, and so it figures you ain't about to — '

'Pretty lady, now you seen and you know,' Smiles said flatly without any change in his expression as he withdrew the threat of the rifle and canted its barrel to his shoulder in a single-handed grip. 'You wanted me to kill you and I sure as hell could have shot your ass off. So if ever *I* want to kill you . . .' He raised his free hand and snapped a finger and thumb. Then swung away from her and while his mouth retained the smile his dark eyes were suddenly coldly menacing as he surveyed the dejected Quinn and the inscrutable Steele – and threatened: 'Man, woman or even child . . . I don't make no differences between them if they got to be killed. Like I said to you before, one of the best.'

'Everyone's making with the mouth, but nobody's telling me a frigging thing I don't already know,' Thorne said, the utter lack of expression on his face and the emptiness of his tone acting to stress the fact that the man was close to the point where he would explode violently free of his present self-restraint.

He was about forty. Five-ten tall and weighing close to a muscular two hundred pounds. Dark-haired with some grey in the sideburns, and dark-eyed. His complexion was dark, too, from a life spent mainly out of doors. All the lines scored into his element-toughened facial flesh were curved in such a way to suggest that he scowled more easily than he grinned.

The Indian-hating Luther Schuler was a few years younger than the top man. A couple of inches taller, but with a much slighter build so he weighed perhaps twenty or even thirty pounds lighter. His hollow-cheeked, sunken-eyed face was also darkenend by hot suns and cold winds. The skin had additionally been ravaged by disease some time ago, and it had been left extensively pocked. His hair was dirty blond and his eyes, which looked to be short-sighted, were somewhere between blue and green. He had too large, tobacco-smoke-stained teeth that made him ugly rather than mean-looking whenever he displayed them between his dry and flaked lips.

Doc Harding was the wrong side of fifty and perhaps getting close to sixty. He was the shortest of the quartet and was the most out of condition, with more flesh than was healthy hung from his belly, at his chest and across his shoulders and rear. What little hair he had left was grey and his skin was a shade of the same neutral colour, his complexion adding to the impression that he was in bad health. He had tiny, animalistic eyes that glittered between red lids, and a cherubic mouth from which the tip of his tongue constantly darted to moisten his lips.

The three white men and the Indian were all attired for riding western trails, and carried holstered revolvers as well as the Winchester rifles. Smiles and Schuler additionally had sheathed knives on their gunbelts. All four horses hitched to the rail had the look of cow ponies and were tacked out with the kind of saddles and accoutrements that pointed to their riders being cowpunchers.

'I think the dude should have his fancy rifle taken away from him, boss,' the Apache said, the smile drifting off his smooth-skinned face now that business was taking over from pleasure.

'He didn't look to have the guts to even think about usin' it — ' Schuler began to sneer, and was interrupted again by Thorne.

'If *I* want these three dead, Charlie, there doesn't seem too much point in having them hand over their guns?'

Amos Quinn had vented a scornful grunt of agreement with Schuler and started to direct a matching gaze at the Virginian. But now became fearful again as he returned his attention to the cold-eyed and monotoned Merle Thorne. This as Mary-Ann groaned in response to a stab of pain, as she remained locked in a private world of misery while she tried to manoeuvre into a more comfortable position on the rock-hard ground.

The Apache hooked the thumb of his free hand and jerked it back up the incline toward the narrowest point between the towering walls of the canyon. Then dropped his hand and patted the closed telescope hanging from his gunbelt. The mime completed, said:

'You tell me to hide up there and to watch, boss. Let you know when Attwood's good friend is getting close. I tell you now, if there's more shooting like there was awhile ago, there's a good chance Attwood's friend and the men guarding him won't come by here.'

'Shit, Injun, you saying' that — '

'Have the dude get down from his horse and see he don't lay a hand on his rifle, Luther,' Thorne instructed. 'Doc, you get to see the old-timer doesn't cause trouble. If either of them even looks like he's about to start stirring shit, give them both what the couple down the well got. And if the shooting scares off . . .' He flicked his gaze from Steele to Quinn and back again and gave an almost imperceptible shrug of his broad shoulders. 'It has to be better than any of us getting blasted. And we can figure out another way.'

'You heard the man, dude!' Schuler snapped, and thrust his rifle toward the Virginian as he gestured with his head.

'Likewise, old man,' Harding said with less aggression in his tone and movements after he reluctantly dragged his gaze away from Mary-Ann.

'Always hoped I'd die quietly,' Quinn said with heavy black sarcasm as he started to climb arthritically down from the wagon after directing a glance of contempt that came close to abhorrence at Steele.

'I'm saying, boss,' the Apache replied to Schuler's unfinished question as the Virginian swung silently down from his saddle, 'that the big man from Europe or wherever must be pretty damn close in the canyon now. No rush yet, I guess, but it won't do any harm to start making things look as they should be soon as you like.'

'I don't carry no weapons,' Quinn growled dispiritedly in response to Harding's hissed demand. And the old-timer raised his arms to the sides and shuffled around in a double about face to confirm that there was no place on his dungaree-clad form where a gun was displayed or could be concealed.

'And a guy like you,' Schuler sneered as he sidestepped toward the stallion after waving Steele away from the animal, 'don't carry no handgun because it'd spoil the way your duds look?' He reached out and, careful to keep his Winchester levelled in a one-handed grip at the Virginian, slid the six shot sporting rifle with the revolving action out of the saddleboot. The sun, near its noonday peak, glinted on the small gold plate screwed to the righthand side of the rosewood stock, and the thin and ugly man interrupted his cautious watch on Steele for long enough to tilt the Colt Hartford and squint at the stock in such a way that he was able to read the inscription on the plate. Then announced: 'His name's Ben Steele and he was give the rifle by old Abe Lincoln.'

'Who friggin' cares?' Harding asked with a shrug.

'I'm Adam Steele,' the Virginian corrected. 'Ben was my father.'

'So, like Doc says, who cares?' the man with a rifle in each hand posed.

'I do, feller.'

'I give a friggin' shit about that?' Schuler muttered.

'Maybe he wants to be sure we get it right on his tombstone?' Harding suggested wryly.

'Doc, get the wagon around to the back someplace!' Thorne ordered impatiently. 'Luther, you take the dude's horse and our mounts out to the corral. Up off your butt, lady. We're all going inside now, and you people better bear this in mind – we all got to die sometime. And sometimes it's left up to us how and when.'

'I'm hoping to get shot dead in bed by the jealous husband of the beautiful woman I just screwed,' the grinning Apache said happily, pointing his rifle at Mary-Ann in a one-handed grip while he extended his free hand in an offer of help.

She glowered at him and shook her head vigorously: a scowl of dislike for the Indian becoming a grimace of pain as she struggled unsteadily to her feet. This as Thorne kept Steele and Quinn carefully covered with his Winchester while Schuler and Harding moved to comply with his instructions.

'Last Apache name I had was Silver Knife,' the garrulous Indian went on in the same light vein as he and the wooden-faced Thorne motioned with their rifles for the prisoners to go into the way station. 'But when I started running with you whites, got called Charlie Smiles. I don't know why the Charlie part, but Smiles because I have a happy-go-lucky nature. Hope to die as happy as I've lived.'

'You won't be the only guy who gets a laugh out of it, Injun,' Schuler growled as he began to unhitch the cow ponies from the rail.

'Always he tries to needle me,' the Apache said softly as he and Thorne crossed the threshold in the wake of the three captives. And there was an underlying tone of irritation in back of the veneer of good humour now. But he managed to suppress the disgruntlement when he swung the door closed on his antagonist and added with a terse laugh: 'I guess because we don't see eye to eye. Hey, you understand . . . needle . . . eye to eye?'

Steele and Quinn turned to face the two men with rifles while Mary-Ann Slattery found her horrified attention trapped by the ugly dark stains, dried brown on the floor, in a patch of sunlight in a corner of the otherwise scrupulously clean room.

'Somebody supposed to say darned if we do?' the Virginian asked flatly.

Smiles vented a harsher gust of laughter and blurted: 'Hey, that's really funny, mister!'

Steele pursed his lips and flicked his mistrustful gaze between the guffawing Apache and the stone-faced Merle Thorne as he drawled: 'So how come you're the only one in stitches, feller?'

FOUR

THE TAINT of black powder-smoke that permeated the atmosphere of the way station's public waiting room to stress that the staining on the floor was caused by the life blood of new dead, and the knowledge among all seven people who now waited tensely within the whitewashed walls that more killing was just the squeeze of a trigger away, acted to dispel any illusion of coolness there might have been from being out from under the direct glare of the harsh noonday sun.

The room took up perhaps a quarter of the building's floor area and had just the one window beside the door, facing onto the trail. There were backless wooden benches along two walls, and three hard-seated armchairs with an adjacent table close to the window. In the rear wall of the room were two doors, both with crudely lettered signs on them – *Private* and *This way to the necessary*. Samplers in frames, needleworked with religious and moral texts, hung on the walls. Along with another hand-lettered sign that requested: *No spitting or profanity please*. There were no rugs on the board floor and a kerosene lamp hung from the centre of the ceiling.

It was just a place where stage passengers could rest in unluxurious but clean and adequately comfortable surroundings while the horse teams were changed. Today, one man held two others and a woman at gunpoint while three others watched from the window for a special and unscheduled stage to come over the crest of the rise between the flanking rock walls of the canyon sides a quarter mile to the north.

The Apache, no longer showing the good humour that had earned him his non-Indian name, sat on the centre of one bench. His rifle rested across his thighs, ready cocked and with a finger curled to the trigger, so that he was constantly just a part of a second away from swinging it toward and firing it at Adam Steele, Amos Quinn or Mary-Ann Slattery who sat in a tight-packed row on the centre of the facing bench across the room: the three crowded close together by order of Smiles rather than from choice. While Thorne, Schuler and Harding ignored the chairs to stand by the window: the top man implacably patient now that the trap was set to be sprung.

'Why were the old folks killed? Anyone answer me that?'

It was the old-timer in the brown dungarees who put the question to end the long silence that had existed since soon after the two men attending to the horses and the wagon had re-entered the way station. By then, the three unwitting intruders and the Apache were already seated on the respective benches, and Thorne was in position at the window – the scowling, muscular man who was the undisputed leader of the ambushers having tacitly given Charlie Smiles responsibility for the prisoners by turning his back on the room. Thorne had additionally demonstrated his trust in the Indian by asking one single, bald question and requiring no qualification of the response.

'How long you figure before they get here, Charlie?'

The Apache answered without time for reflection: 'Thirty minutes or so, boss. If they keep coming the way they were when I saw them last.'

Then Schuler and Harding came into the way station, the tall and ugly man smoking a foul-smelling cigarette that for awhile acted to mask the stink of death that clung to the room. He was silently malcontent with the changed situation caused by the unexpected arrival of the newcomers, and continued to share his tacit displeasure equally among them and the Apache who had brought them here. While the short, fat, grey-faced Harding – resigned to being denied his pleasure with the widow woman – found himself provoked to rising uneasiness by the presence of the impassive Steele, the morose Quinn and the withdrawn Mary-Ann Slattery. And it was he who demanded to know:

'Well, Charlie, you ready to let us in on the secret of why we got company when the last thing we friggin' need is company?'

Only the lip-licking Harding, and the Virginian who made no pretence of not listening to the Apache's reply, appeared to be interested in what was said by the brave, who never allowed his attention to wander away from his charges. And, as he answered the question, Smiles looked longer and harder at Steele than at Quinn beside him and the woman on the other side of the old-timer – like he was eager to see how the Virginian reacted to the explanation.

'I spotted them soon as I went up there into the north section of the canyon. Saw through the glass that it wasn't the bunch we wanted. Saw, too, that they didn't look like they'd stir up any trouble for us. So I just stayed down behind the rocks and planned to let them go on by – for the boss to take care of however he wanted. Have to say, though: the nearer they got and the more I saw of the dude close up, the more careful I knew I had to be to keep him from seeing me.'

He paused, in implied invitation for Steele to confirm what he suspected. But the Virginian merely inclined his head in the slightest of nods – elected not to reveal to the arrogant young brave that he would have been enduring a bad bout of self-doubt and maybe anger had anyone but an Indian remained hidden to him for so long in such circumstances. Smiles seemed to be disdainful of what he assumed to be faint praise, but then made it apparent that he was going to be critical of his partners in the impending ambush when he scowled briefly at them as he continued:

'After the three of them had gone by me, I was almost sure I had my first sight of the stage. But the mist of heat was gathering and I couldn't be certain. Even with the glass. Then, as I saw the stage for sure, I heard the gunfire from down here. I knew these three had heard it, also. But not the people with the stage, far as I could tell from what I saw in the glass. By the time I got into position to make these prisoners, the stage was closer. Almost close enough to see without the glass. I figured those with the stage couldn't see the wagon though, because of the shadow of the canyon wall. But it does not matter – unless they are blind they will have seen wagon tracks in dust of trail. But if they are close enough to hear gunfire this time . . .'

The Apache shrugged the implication that his actions beyond this point were self-explanatory. Thorne, who had his back to the room and so did not see the gesture, revealed he had been listening to what was said when he growled:

'Good thinking, Charlie. We should have given it as much thought before blasting the crazy old bastard and his missus.'

Like he was anxious to have the subject changed, the fleshy and unhealthy looking Harding snarled hastily: 'Cats can get skinned lotsa ways.'

'You want to have the use of my knife, Doc?' the Apache invited. 'Or you figure you can do it with your bare hands? How about a sack or a pillow or something to smother them with? Beat them over the head until . . . shit, how you going to stop the other two raising hell while you're taking care of the first — '

'Not now, Goddamnit!' the discomfited Harding cut in defensively. 'I mean when you had them where you wanted them and they didn't know it! You're an Apache. I thought your kind were the best at creepin' up on people and stickin' in the knife or whatever before the people know what's friggin' happenin'?'

'That's bullshit, Doc,' Schuler growled sourly.

'Well, the way Charlie is always braggin' . . .' Harding countered.

Then, as he exchanged a glance with the taller and thinner man and both of them eyed the broad back of the taciturn Merle Thorne with matching expressions of something close to resentment, the complaining fat man decided to let the subject rest. And thus began the lengthy silence of perhaps three or four minutes that Amos Quinn ended with his query about the killing of the couple whose corpses were in the bottom of the well.

For several stretched seconds, it seemed that the question was going to remain unanswered – when none of the men gazing from the window gave any indication that he heard what had been said. Then, in the familiar dispassionate monotone, Thorne replied without interrupting his cautious surveillance on the narrow point of the canyon:

'On account of we aren't so clear-headed and cool-thinking as Charlie, old man. It never should have been. Plan was for the oldsters to sit still and quiet like you people until we'd finished our business with the stage and got the hell out of here. For awhile after we saw you and the wagon up there at the top of the slope, it seemed like that was what was going to happen. But I think maybe you stayed sitting up there too long. Got on the oldsters' nerves – not knowing if you planned to come on down or turn around and head back the way you came. Old lady bounced to her feet and made a dash for the door. Her old man either tried to stop her or planned to go with her. Can't say who fired the first shot. Maybe me. Or Luther or Doc. Don't matter a damn right now. Got them out of our hair. Figured Charlie would take care of you after you decided to turn tail and get the hell away when you saw us get rid of the corpses. Like I say, it wasn't part of the plan but . . .'

Now he shrugged, and left a sentence incomplete.

'Same as you people weren't ever a part of it, either,' Schuler said pointedly, and emphasized his meaning with a menacing scowl as he added: 'So if you get outta line, you know just what's gonna — '

'Hey, Merle!' Harding rasped, his voice suddenly tremulous with nervous excitement.

'I see them, Doc,' Thorne answered tonelessly. 'Luther, make less with the mouth and do what you have to with the dude and the old-timer. Charlie, bring the woman to the door.'

'What I have to, Merle?' Schuler asked croakily, his deeply-pocked face expressing confusion.

Thorne vented a short and noisy sigh and glanced away from the window to rake the tension-charged room with a brief look of cold anger: before he returned his gaze to the scene out in the canyon to which the frightened fat man had needlessly called his attention.

'If they get out of line, kill them is what I mean,' the leader of the ambushers explained, making it clear that he resented the need to elaborate on planning what was clear in his own mind. 'I'm going to use the woman as a lever and if either of those two try to stop me, kill them. And we'll fall back on the way we planned it at first. All right?'

'Yeah, Merle,' Harding confirmed eagerly, and began to lick his lips more rapidly as he took a firmer grip on his rifle and seemed to be unable to tear his fascinated gaze away from the tableau out on the trail.

The Apache had already risen to his feet and advanced halfway across the room. He held his Winchester in a one-handed grip around the frame, forefinger curled to the trigger and muzzle aimed at the left breast of Mary-Ann Slattery. Now he drew the knife from its sheath on his gunbelt and wreathed his handsome face with a grin of evil delight as he gently tapped the flat of the blade against his right cheek.

'Okay, Merle,' Schuler growled, trying to look and sound confident in his ability to do what was asked of him as he side-stepped quickly from the window to the rear wall of the room between the two doors. He kept his rifle levelled from the hip and expressed something akin to relief when he got to the position he sought without having Thorne criticize him.

Then the clop of hooves and the clatter of wheelrims against the compacted dirt of the trail reached into the sunlit, oppressively hot room: and it seemed to be this body of familiar sound rather than anything which was happening inside the way station that acted to jolt the woman from her trance-like state.

'You scream, all die,' the Apache warned, the smile wavering for just a moment as he recognized the depth of terror in the blue eyes of Mary-Ann Slattery.

Just a muted groan emerged from her constricted throat as she looked to left and right – like somebody newly-awakened from a lengthy sleep. Then, fully aware of where she was and comforted to an extent to know that Quinn and Steele were still close at hand, she was able to regain full, if not entirely firm, self-control.

'What do they want?' she asked, head turned toward the old-timer and, beyond him, the Virginian.

'They plan to — ' Quinn began.

'Hurry it up, Charlie!' Thorne snapped with impatience impairing his attempt to seem coldly composed as the sounds of the moving rig and its escorting riders rose in volume.

Everyone except for the Apache glanced toward the abruptly anxious Thorne and the patently afraid Harding who peered unceasingly out of the window. Until all attention was in an instant directed at Smiles and Mary-Ann. Drawn to them by the Indian's sudden lunge forward, the woman's choked cry of alarm and then his soft-spoken command:

'Up on your feet, pretty lady.'

The woman did as she was told, her head held at an unnatural upward tilt by fear of, rather than pressure of, the knife-blade that was held under her chin. The Apache's rifle was held negligently down at his side now, posing no threat to anyone: and the contentedly smiling brave continued to concern himself only with Mary-Ann as he issued her with tacit orders that she obeyed at once as the sounds of the horses and a wagon got louder by the moment. With the expression in his eyes, gestures of his head and slight movements of the dangerously-positioned knife, the Indian had her move with him as he backed away from the two men who remained motionless on the bench. Then, the beads of sweat squeezing from her pores the only sign of animation in her mask-like face, she slowly turned her back on the brave as he moved up close against her. And so he was in total control of her – the movements she made and their directions dictated by his own as he held the knife blade across her throat in a hand resting over her right shoulder while he angled up the Winchester to level it beside her left hip.

'Get the door for him, Doc,' Thorne said tensely. 'Open it when I say.'

He was watching the trail again.

The lip-licking little fat man looked about to question the instruction, but sensed the dangerous extent of latent tension simmering just below the surface of the man, and so backed into a position where he would be able to do what was asked of him.

On the far side of the room from the jittery Harding, Schuler blinked his shortsighted eyes as he tried vainly to concentrate his attention on Adam Steele and Amos Quinn – but found himself unable to resist the impulse to direct frequent glances at the door that gave on to the way station's private quarters.

Quinn constantly shifted his gaze about the room in fear and frustration, until he felt himself trapped into staring with fixed intensity at the strangely calm woman and her smiling Apache captor who had come to a halt just far enough back from the door so that it could be wrenched open when the time came by the now visibly quaking Harding.

The Virginian, too, kept altering the direction and focus of his dark-eyed gaze so that he was constantly aware of each small change in the volatile situation that got more dangerous with each part of a second that passed. He was as sweatingly afraid as everyone else within the confines of the room, but sought to use fear as a hone on his reflexes. And he felt, also, much the same degree of helplessness as prisoners and guards alike while they all waited for somebody outside to trigger an action that would spark necessary reaction. But such frustration could not be adapted to a positive purpose and Steele could only seek to check the feeling and struggle against it developing into futile and perhaps reckless anger.

'Steele?' Amos Quinn rasped and the monosyllable sounded like a sobbing cry for help from a man drowning in a morass of depression.

The Virginian glanced at the old man and saw that he was still staring in terrified fascination at the woman and the Indian. Then saw, beyond Quinn's motionless profile, that Luther Schuler was peering with the same degree of unswerving directness at the door, beyond which was relief from the unbearable tension that had built up in this room. And as he saw the man with the pock-marked face begin to seriously consider making a break for it, Steele started to scratch his right leg – moving the gloved fingers down his thigh to his knee and then leaned forward a little so that he could reach for his calf.

'Prepare to halt . . . halt!' a man familiar with being in authority yelled.

Other men, equally familiar with the vagaries of equine responses to commands, augmented the movement of reins with raucously spoken words to bring the animals to a stop, and thus altered the tone and cadence and then curtailed the sounds from outside the way station.

In perhaps two full seconds of utter silence inside and out of the building, the Virginian knew that Schuler, had he not been petrified by fear, would have made his lunge for escape through the nearest door. And in that same brief period, Steele remained poised to delve his right hand into the slit in the outside of his right pants leg. Had planned only far enough ahead to the point where he slid the knife from the boot sheath and brought it out into the open. Just who he would send the finely balanced, sharply honed weapon spinning toward depended upon which man presented the major threat as he powered for the door opened by Schuler.

And the hell with Mary-Ann Slattery and Amos Quinn . . .

'Now, Doc!' Merle Thorne said softly. And shoved his Winchester forward: jerked it back as soon as the thrusting muzzle had shattered the window pane.

With a sound that came close to being a sob, Doc Harding pulled the door violently open and leapt backwards to ensure he was clear of the threshold.

With a composure that probably seemed more ice cold than it was because of the uncompromising manner in which Thorne and Harding made their presence known to the newcomers, the Apache eased Mary-Ann in to the doorway and remained as close to her as before.

This as Luther Schuler overcame the compulsion to turn tail and run – stared and aimed his rifle exclusively at Steele in a way that made it appear he had read what was in the mind of the man who continued to scratch the side of his knee.

'Captain!' a man outside rasped. 'He's got a knife on her!'

Mary-Ann uttered a low and plaintive whine, like that of a mournful dog.

'He's a friggin' Injun!' another man blurted.

'Reach, soldier boys!' Thorne ordered. 'Or the lady is all through with living.'

'Captain, you better do — '

'I don't take orders from a trooper!' the man in command cut in stridently. 'And I am not responsible for any civilian other than the — '

Although he could not be entirely certain that Luther Schuler was in control of himself and would not start firing at the prisoners out of unreasoning panic, Adam Steele found that he was unable to resist a compulsion to turn and look at the scene outside – those component parts of it that were visible through the shattered window and the open door that were further obscured by the forms of Thorne and the Apache and the woman.

Amos Quinn, who was already staring past Mary-Ann Slattery at where the blue-clad cavalry captain sat his horse some twenty feet beyond the threshold of the room, caught his breath and clasped his gnarled and skinny hands tightly together at his narrow chest before he groaned: 'Dear God in heaven, what next?'

This as the trooper who was being bawled out by the captain withdrew the Spencer carbine from its boot on his saddle and took aim from the shoulder at the nape of the unsuspecting officer's neck. And Steele shifted his narrow-eyed gaze to the window, beyond which the Concord coach of the Texas-California Transport Company was halted. From which there began to emerge an elderly man who was able to maintain a great deal of natural dignity, despite being anxiously disconcerted by the tableau of impending violence of which he was an intrinsic part.

As the elegantly attired, ramrod-stiff passenger lowered a leading foot on to the top step below the swinging open door, the captain sensed the threat from an unexpected quarter and interrupted himself before he slowly turned his head to look at the aimed gun. And the Virginian responded to Quinn evenly:

'Reckon we should take it one stage at a time.'

FIVE

THE CAVALRY captain who was closer to fifty than forty and probably stood more than six feet tall, looked to be every inch a military man with many years service behind him. His element-burnished and time-scored face did not alter in expression as his clear blue eyes confirmed his suspicion that one of his detail was aiming a gun at his head. And then, as he became aware of the elderly passenger descending from the stage, the look of implacable resignation to each new turn of events was abruptly mixed with a quota of professional deference as he pointedly ignored everyone else present to request:

'I'd be obliged, sir, if you will remain aboard until I and my men have taken care of this matter.'

The man who now stood on the trail beside the Concord seemed to relish being on solid ground after spending so long inside the jolting stage. And used a few moments to gently flex his travel-wearied muscles while he scanned his surroundings. Then, in a tone of voice that was ill-matched to his elegant appearance, he squinted up at the carbine-threatened officer and answered: 'You want I shouldn't have the pleasure of seeing you get your foolish head shot off, Captain McClure?'

'Sure'll be my pleasure to do that, Count,' the man with the Spencer aimed at McClure's neck offered.

The two of these had been riding out ahead of the stage. A sergeant had the reins of the four-horse team with a corporal up on the high seat beside him. And two more troopers had ridden drag. One of the men at the rear shot a covert glance at the second and made to cautiously draw his carbine from the boot. But the man who had appeared to agree to a surprise counter-move against the ambushers abruptly abandoned the pretext of secrecy – jerked out his carbine and aimed it so that the muzzle touched the neck of his fellow trooper just below his ear.

'Captain!' the tricked man wailed as he allowed his own gun to drop back into the boot, and froze.

Steele could not see from his restricted viewpoint what was happening at the rear of the stalled stage. But he recognized the despair in the single word and saw shock expressed by the sergeant and corporal as they half-turned on the seat to see a second trooper reveal he was allied with the ambushers. At the same time as the civilian passenger looked in the same direction and appeared unsurprised, while McClure's composure began to show signs of strain.

'I can't say I'm exactly astonished at you, Ehrman,' he said sneeringly of the man threatening him, as he attempted to hide just how badly he had been shaken. 'But I thought more highly of you, Greg Priest.'

'Shit, Merle, who gives a frig for what that uppity, high-hatty bastard thinks about Frank and Greg?' Schuler demanded from the rear wall of the way station room, his anxiety with the situation pushing his voice toward almost feminine shrillness. 'Let's get this friggin' scheme — '

'Now that we all know where we all stand in this thing,' Thorne cut in evenly on the disconcerted man behind him, 'I was about to tell all you people to make less with the mouth. And do like you're told. First of all, you soldiers get rid of the carbines and the pistols. Easy out of where they're at and toss them over to the far side of the trail.'

'Count Zucconi, I — ' McClure started.

'I'll kill you, shithead!' Thorne warned with a flare of impatience, and shifted the aim of his rifle from the civilian to the officer.

'And I'll cut her from ear to ear, soldier boy,' the Apache added: caused Mary-Ann Slattery to moan in expectation of sudden death as he slightly altered the position of the knife against her throat.

After sitting as immobile as a carved statue for many stretched seconds, the old man on the bench beside Steele now uttered a sound like an echo of the woman's cry as his frame became limp and he slumped back against the hard wall. Not passed out, but utterly drained of the will to take an active part in the explosive situation that got to be more tension-filled with each split second the captain refused to order a surrender.

'Tell your men to lay down their arms,' Count Zucconi advised, and now that his title and name had been announced and he spoke with an earnest tone, the Virginian detected a slight foreign accent in back of the man's more pronounced New England timbre.

'I'm charged to put your safety above and beyond every other consideration during this mission, sir, and — '

'They have no intention of harming me, Captain,' Zucconi interrupted as Schuler began to mutter a string of obscenities that probably did not carry outside of the way station. 'For the time being. And if it was just you and the men under your command who were in danger, perhaps I would not be so insistent. But since that innocent woman's life is — '

'How do we know she's innocent?' McClure demanded stiffly of the foreigner. Then eyed Mary-Ann and the Apache with derision as he added: 'She could be with them like Ehrman and Priest and simply play-acting to — '

'Cut her open, Charlie,' Thorne ordered icily.

The woman seemed until now to have resigned herself to her fate with the same degree of uncomplaining passivity as Quinn. But the coldly-spoken words of the man at the smashed window penetrated deep enough to touch her basic instinct for self-preservation. And she opened her mouth to its widest extent – like she needed to power her doomed attempt at escape with sound. Managed to start the piercingly shrill scream and to bunch her muscles in readiness to try to wrench free of the Indian's grasp. Then was instantly silent and unmoving. Like everyone else except for Captain McClure. In the wake of a single rifle shot that exploded a bullet into the officer's brow a little to the right of centre, killed him as it drove through his brain and burst clear at the crown of his head to spray the inside of his uniform cap with blood and gore as it displaced it. Dead in the saddle, McClure's body seemed to remain upright for an inordinate length of time, before it swayed to the right, became limp and slithered to the ground beside his horse that moved disdainfully away.

'No need to kill her now, Merle?' Doc Harding asked, his tone sounding brittle as he pumped the lever action of the Winchester to eject the spent cartridge case in a spinning arc and jack a fresh bullet into the breech.

'Boss?' the Apache asked, and sounded as tense as the short, fat man at his side as the both of them tracked their rifles to aim them at the suddenly sick-looking non-coms on the seat of the Concord.

Ehrman and Priest, and the trooper who was covered by Priest, were also abruptly more uneasy after the killing.

'Merle, you said we'd try to do this without anybody gettin' hurt?' Ehrman complained – and abruptly booted his carbine in a manner that clearly stated he had no intention of killing anyone.

'Just if the three guys with guns haven't done as I told them before I've finished talking, Charlie,' Thorne told the Apache. And when Zucconi swung to left and right to direct pleading looks up at the men on the high seat and the one astride a horse, all three of them began to discard their weapons – over-emphasizing every move to ensure the ambushers saw there was no intention of attempting to put up a fight. This while Thorne went on for the attention of all who might draw comfort from what the trooper had said: 'Was the idea at the start sure enough, Frank. But the way things turned out, Doc and Luther and me had to kill the old couple that used to run this place. And it didn't bother any of us. Appears Doc got a taste for it.'

'Shit, better that duty-first-and-last shithead officer than the woman, Merle. Like I said right at the start after Charlie got the drop on them, she could do a lot to help the time pass — '

'That's fine,' Thorne announced, ignoring Harding to voice his response to the discarding of carbines and revolvers by the submissive soldiers. 'Turn her loose, Charlie. Then you and Doc step outside. Okay, Luther, you can go on through to the back now. Guess you aren't so scared yellow anymore that you'll forget to lock the door after you?'

'Aw, Merle, I never — ' Schuler began, but was driven into

shame-faced silence by the harsh expression of boundless contempt which Thorne directed at him.

This as Harding moved across the threshold of the front door and the Apache – his smile suddenly tinged with sadness – slowly turned, and with something close to gentleness withdrew the threat of the knife from Mary-Ann Slattery.

Schuler was much more hurried than either of the other men as he swung open the door to the way station's private quarters, slid through and banged it closed. After the key was heard to turn in the lock, the scowling Thorne gestured with his Winchester and snapped at the woman who remained in the doorway precisely as the brave had left her:

'Move across to join your friends.'

She stood as inert as Amos Quinn sat. Her shoulders slumped, her hands hanging down at her sides and her slender body looking to be on the point of corkscrewing to the floor as her legs ceased to support her. But her head was held high, so that she was able to peer unblinkingly into whatever images were created against the infinity that was their backdrop. Her pale face, sheened with sweat between the dishevelled strands of her blonde hair, was blank of expression, and she was obviously detached from her surroundings again – oblivious to what Thorne said to her and the look of menace that was set firmer on his element-scarred features when she failed to obey him.

Then Quinn groaned in helpless frustration again. And Thorne whirled toward the bench, his rifle aimed at Adam Steele as the Virginian rose to his feet.

'You want to go down the well with the others?' the leader of the ambushers snarled, as angry at himself for reacting so nervously as he was at the Virginian for causing him to reveal the extent of his anxiety.

'I'm not that crazy, feller,' Steele answered evenly, and moved with wary slowness across the room toward Mary-Ann, dividing his cautious attention between the woman who was totally unaware of him and the man with the rifle who watched him with a kind of pained apprehension. 'Just unbalanced enough to risk my neck to help a lady in distress this much?'

He reached her side and as he turned and curled an arm around her waist, glanced outside and saw the Apache grinning enthusiastically at him.

'Had him covered every inch of the way, boss,' the brave said, and leaned in over the threshold to show his happiness-wreathed face and levelled rifle.

Beyond him, Harding, Ehrman and Priest were urging the trio of captive cavalrymen down off the stage and from the saddle and forming them into a group with the civilian who continued to be the most unruffled man outside of the way station.

Merle Thorne adopted anger as an ineffective defensive cover for anxiety, and snarled: 'Anybody else does a frigging thing without being told to, he's for the well!'

The woman suddenly became conscious of being in the embrace of a man again. And this knowledge jolted her out of the reverie that had kept her immune from the ill effects of her circumstances for almost a full minute. She stared at Steele for a moment, then wrenched her head around to peer at Thorne and Smiles. Non-comprehension changed to understanding on her strained features. But delayed shock as she recalled what had happened before barred her from thinking a single step beyond the scene that she witnessed now. Her body trembled against his arm and Steele tightened his hold as he told her:

'You're safe enough, Mrs Slattery. Just take it easy and — '

He had thought she was on the verge of collapsing into a faint. But suddenly he felt a new strength charge her slender frame. And he was nonplussed as she powered free of his grip, dashed across the room and flung herself down on the bench beside Amos Quinn: looked to be close to weeping until she took one of his hands in both of hers. The old-timer smiled and brought his other hand to complete the four-part clasp. And then, despite looking drained and defeated, there suddenly showed in his weary eyes an expression of deeply-felt pride. While Mary-Ann stared with defiance out of despair. Both apportioning their emotions equally among Steele, Thorne and the Apache.

'Seems she's the kind of female who prefers older men, dude,'

Merle Thorne growled, in a manner that suggested he considered he was scoring a point off the Virginian.

'But the dude seems like the kind who doesn't give a damn,' Smiles added indifferently.

Steele nodded as the two men with rifles backed away outside. And, his mind drifting back to a shack on a hillside outside of a Texas town, he gazed levelly at the woman and murmured: 'Reckon it's way past time for me to start caring.'

SIX

THE MAN who introduced himself as Count Paulo Zucconi was about sixty years old. He was tall and leanly built, with a maturely good-looking face that was darkly tanned, so that his slicked down hair appeared to be as white as his even teeth, and his clear blue eyes seemed to sparkle with exceptional brightness. Although he had been travel-stained by sweat and dust from a lengthy ride aboard the stage, and probably was shaken more than he showed by the ambush and the killing of Captain McClure, the no-longer-young Italian aristocrat was quick to recover his composure as he brushed and shook the dust from his elegant city suit and Stetson, and then rubbed the tacky salt moisture off his face and the nape of his neck with a linen handkerchief.

He began to repair his dishevelled appearance as he was herded into the way station with the three loyal soldiers, and Steele saw at once that the man was using his apparent fastidious preoccupation with his appearance as a distraction behind which he struggled to settle his jangled nerves. Then, when the man entered the room, the soldiers respectfully holding back to allow the civilian to go first despite the harrying guns of Ehram, Priest and Harding, he saw the Virginian was watching him and began immediately to talk too quickly, as an additional barrier behind which he sought to conceal his true feelings.

'I am from that region of Italy which is called Tuscany,' he rushed on after announcing his name as the front door of the way station was flung closed and the key was turned in the lock. 'Near to the town of Siena in the district of Chianti where the grapes for the world-famous wine are grown. But I have spent much time in your country. In the cities of New York and Boston and Chicago and Philadelphia. Washington, too, of course. And many other areas of the United States I visit. On behalf of my country and its government. Seeking to increase our trade with your country. I am called a special envoy, but I am really not so special, although Cornelius Attwood will probably consider otherwise and will pay these bandits what they demand if it is reasonable. So, I hope, you will not have to endure this discomfort for too much longer time because certain people have an inflated opinion of my importance.'

'Count, is there any particular place you'd—' the stockily-built, square-featured, red-headed and doleful-eyed sergeant asked.

'Please forget about my title of rank, Sergeant,' the Italian cut in, and was less perturbed now – perhaps because Steele had turned his attention to what was happening beyond the shattered window. 'And I wish you all to do the same. People say, when in Rome, do as the Romans do. I have been to Rome only twice in my entire life. In the United States where there is so little standing on ceremony, I spend many years. My given name of Paulo is the same as Paul. I would like for you all to call me this, if you will.

'Now I introduce to you, Sergeant Delany, Corporal Rivers and Trooper Wade who, to my embarrassment, would certainly have died in an attempt to protect me if the unfortunate Captain McClure had insisted upon placing duty above reason.'

'Sir, I guess I'm in command of the military now the captain's gone,' the thirty-or-so-years-old Delany said deferentially. 'And, beggin' your pardon, sir, I feel I got to run my end of things like he would've, Count?'

The short and skinny, blond-headed Rivers and the tall and broadly built, bushy-moustached Wade, who were both in their mid-twenties, bobbed their heads in agreement with what was said.

'I'm Mrs Mary-Ann Slattery and this is Mr Amos Quinn,' the woman told the Italian in a toneless voice that matched the drained look on her face. And added, with just a hint of enmity when all four newcomers glanced toward the man at the window: 'That's Mr Adam Steele. We were travelling together before we became involved in this affair.'

Although the ill-feeling directed toward the Virginian by the widow woman's tone and the old-timer's expression was restrained by weariness rather than inclination, it was still plainly heard and seen.

'Was fixin' to ask, sir,' the senior non-com hurried on as Zucconi did a double take between the bench and the window, 'if there was some particular place you'd like to sit? The chairs look a whole lot more comfortable than the benches and — '

'I'm neither a baby nor a senile old man, Sergeant,' the count interrupted. 'And I'd appreciate it if you'd stop fussing over me as though I were one or the other.'

'Whatever you say, sir.'

Delany gestured for the other two cavalrymen to take seats on the bench across the room from where Mary-Ann and Quinn were sitting. Then went to stand to one side of Steele as the Italian came to a halt on the other side, Zucconi placing the Stetson back on his head now that it was brushed free of dust and the introductions were completed.

'You were riding a mount and your . . . companions were aboard a heavy-loaded wagon, Mr Steele?' the sergeant posed.

'Had no reason to hide our sign, feller.'

'Somebody on foot stopped you up at the top of the hill where the canyon gets real narrow and came on down here with you?'

'Stopped up there by choice to watch what was happening at this place,' the Virginian corrected without surliness. 'Heard three of them shoot the people who ran the way station and saw them drop the bodies in the well at the side. Then the Apache jumped us.'

'Ain't no Injun sneakier than an Apache, unless it be a Comanche I reckon,' the non-com growled, in a manner that suggested he was anxious not to be thought critical of Steele's actions.

'You listen to me, soldier boy,' Charlie Smiles called cheerfully from where he squatted against the wall on the far side of the door from the window. 'Even the worst brave of the Apache nation is better than the best Comanche.'

Surprised that one of their captors was close enough to eavesdrop, Sergeant Delany vented a low snort of anger and leaned forward to thrust his head between the viciously-pointed shards of glass that still remained in the frame after Merle Thorne's rifle muzzle had shattered the pane. But he quickly straightened up and jerked his head inside when the Apache made a threatening gesture with his Winchester before he warned:

'If you're tired of living with all your new responsibility, soldier boy, stick your ugly mug out of the window once more. You understand me?'

'Or you can try gettin' out through this way!' Luther Schuler yelled jeeringly from beyond the door he had locked. 'If you prefer a white man instead of an Injun to end it all for you!'

Delany and Zucconi exchanged worried frowns in response to learning that they were being listened to as well as guarded at both front and rear.

The Apache spat forcefully in angry reaction to the latest implied slight against his race. Then raised his voice to retort: 'The boss sure knew what he was doing when he put a piece of shit like you in the back passage, Schuler!'

The three men in back of the broken window saw the familiar scowl on the face of Thorne develop briefly into a grin as his favourite member of the bunch scored a verbal point against the one he liked least. But his good humour was short-lived as he directed the softly muttering Harding and the pair of more willing troopers in the chores necessary to put the next phase of the plan into operation.

'Captain McClure was right,' Delany growled in a harsh whisper that was probably heard by the Apache, but did not carry to where the uniformed men were preparing to move the stage and saddle horses around to the rear of the way station, and Harding was wrapping the corpse of the officer in a blanket. 'Ain't a man on the post'll be surprised to hear that Frank Ehrman is mixed up in this rotten business. But Greg Priest, I'd have thought he'd be the last man at the fort to run with skunks like these.'

Steele, the major part of his consciousness still concerned with times and places recalled by the woman's attitude toward him and the wry comments this had drawn from others, remained aware of his present surroundings and what was taking place there. So heard what the stocky, square-faced non-com said and reflected absently that the opinion twice expressed was obviously based upon the men's facades. For Ehrman was tall and broad and had a sun-burnished face that had probably been ugly before the nose was broken and the scar tissue formed above his right eye and on his left cheek close to the ear. Whereas Priest, who was a match for the other trooper's late-twenties age, was almost a head shorter and perhaps weighed less than half what Ehrman did. And he had weakly handsome features, a quality emphasised by the paleness of his complexion and a strangely forlorn quality that emanated from his soft brown eyes when his expression was in repose. Steele, even though he was mainly concerned with events in the more distant past, was still able to recall how patches of colour had blazed on Priest's wan cheeks and a glitter of viciousness came to his eyes as he held his carbine against the neck of his fellow trooper.

The period in his past upon which the Virginian superficially dwelled after each dangerous plan of escape had been rejected was that in which Amos Quinn and, particularly, Mary-Ann Slattery figured. And as he watched the men outside undertake the chores dictated by Thorne, and listened to the Italian make apologies for the trouble he had caused, Adam Steele reached a decision about his relationship with the former owner of the grocery and notions store in Barclay Texas and the new widow.

What had happened in the store and the manner in which he had become involved in the later tragedy of the woman he found so sexually attractive would not, in the usual circumstances of his life, have caused him to do any soul-searching. Or, at least, he would have forgotten what old man Quinn looked like within hours of riding away from the violence in that Texas town: and only on the most forlorn of lonesome nights would he have experienced aching remorse that he failed to make use of Mary-Ann's fine body that had surely been offered him. Offered him, albeit, at a time when the woman was confronted from the depths of fresh grief by a future of loneliness in a hostile environment.

Until recently, the Virginian had been close to being the kind of man who might have submitted to the temptation of accepting what life proffered without thought of the repercussions for himself or anybody else. But, before he plunged fully to this depth of degradation, he had resolved to abandon his drifting life and put down roots. To attempt to create something out here in the West that bore a passing resemblance to the birthright he had lost long ago in far off Virginia.

To this end, he had his sights set on a studfarm. And in the hip pocket of his pants right now he had in excess of four thousand dollars with which he hoped to get started on this latest dream he was determined to make a reality. There had been more, shortly after the seeds of his ambition to breed fine horses on a fine spread had begun to germinate. But the fates had sought to keep him from doing what he wanted, and a man had to live while he rode with life's punches and waited for the breaks.

Always before, he had eventually bent to the will of what had seemed an inevitable destiny of drifting into and fighting his way out of other people's troubles. But then the ambition had never been so clear-cut – had consisted of some pipe-dreamed castle in the air to which it had been impossible to cling tenaciously enough when the fates conspired to work violently against him. Whereas this time . . . he had even got so far as to buy two first-class stallions with which to start his stud. He didn't have them anymore, but the cruel manner in which he lost them had not caused him to lose sight of his aim. And his resolve to succeed in achieving this aim remained as firm as ever throughout the trouble that involved him with Amos Quinn and Mary-Ann Slattery.

Then had come their meeting on the trail that led to this fresh outbreak of violence in this canyon of death. When, at the start, Steele had found it refreshingly relaxing to talk about his plans to the pair of interested and then eager listeners. Had been so absorbed in the plans he vocalized for the first time that he failed to perceive that he was allowing his two companions to become part of what he was talking about: until this very morning when he abruptly faced up to the obvious . . .

That he was a self-sufficient man of an age to have ample years left to fulfil a time-honed ambition. While his companions were rootless wanderers who had each left a bridge blazing back at Barclay. One an old man too much wearied by life to start up in business for himself again, and the other an unattached woman with virtually no experience of living out on the frontier. And he and these two, without any actual words on the subject being spoken, had become inextricably enmeshed in his plan for the future.

While Adam Steele was pondering his involvement with the old-timer and the woman, the corpse of McClure was fully wrapped in the blanket by the grimacing Doc Harding and then, with the assistance of Thorne, was draped over and lashed to the saddle of the captain's own gelding. And Priest and Ehrman took the stage off the trail and around to the corral out back of the way station. From where sounds of the team horses being unharnessed and taken into the stable for feed and water could be heard. This as the now totally composed European aristocrat explained in an almost penitent manner:

'Although it was always possible that an event such as this would mar my first visit to the south-western territories of your country, there was a limit to what counter-measures could be taken to guard against it. I considered the size of the escort adequate and I certainly had no reason to suspect any member of the guard of being disloyal.'

'It's just that Frank Ehrman's always been a trouble-maker, sir,' Sergeant Delany cut in bitterly.

'It serves no purpose to examine any predicament with benefit of hindsight,' Zucconi said to check whatever else the non-com at his side had it in mind to add. Then glanced at Steele who flanked him on the other side and Quinn and Mary-Ann who continued to sit close together on one of the benches. 'But it does, perhaps, help by some small degree to ease the burden of danger and discomfort if all those who are enduring it know the reason for it?'

'I'm sure you're right, Count,' the woman offered.

'Guess it won't do no harm, Mr Zucconi,' Quinn added.

'*Buono*. Good. As I told you earlier, I am a trade envoy to your country from Italy. Once I have established the openings through which the raw materials and the manufactured goods may be traded, my purpose is fulfilled. But sometimes men who do business together become friends. Such friends did Cornelius Attwood and I become. You know of this famous man, no doubt?'

Quinn growled: 'One of the sonofbitches that got us locked up in here made mention of him.'

'I suppose it's the same Mr Attwood who is the railroad baron, Count?' Mary-Ann suggested, her tone not quite indifferent.

'You are correct, *signora*. Cornelius Attwood is a railroadman of high fame in the east of your country. Less well known out in the territories perhaps: because his business interests are almost exclusively in the east. But he does have a ranch in this area. Known as North Bend — '

'Or to those that work there,' the Apache interrupted evenly from outside, 'as Arizona's Asshole.'

Zucconi pulled a face, but checked an impulse to respond to Charlie Smiles and continued in the same tone as before: 'It was to North Bend that Mr Attwood invited me for a visit. And to which I was on my way when this unfortunate incident that has involved you innocent people took place.' He would perhaps have finished at this point, but now he vented a muted grunt of mild satisfaction as an idea occurred to him. And he murmured: 'An unfortunate incident, it would seem, caused by men with real or imagined reason to hold a grudge against Cornelius Attwood.'

'Real enough, mister!' the Apache supplied, softly but with a great deal of venom.

'Those inside are making enough with the mouth for all of us, Charlie,' Merle Thorne said with faint rebuke, as Troopers Ehrman and Priest reappeared on the trail out front of the way station, the taller, scar-faced cavalryman leading one of the army horses. But it was the pale and skinny, weakly handsome Greg Priest who swung smoothly up into the saddle, and accepted the lead line on the corpse-burdened gelding from Doc Harding.

And Steele decided to give himself no more opportunities to reconsider the decision he had reached about his relationship with Amos Quinn and Mary-Ann Slattery – a relationship which he was only prepared to acknowledge until the trouble in which they were all involved was ended. Maybe, he had reflected, if there had been no ambush and killing he would, by early this afternoon, have severed his ties with the old-timer and the widow woman. Be long gone on his faster horse while they trundled along the uneventful trail in no need – as far as he was aware – of help and protection. But, just as the Italian count had said, there was little point in bringing hindsight to bear on the present trouble.

They had been a group when the Apache captured them: and no matter what they had felt then or how they saw it now, by his own code he considered himself responsible for them. And so, unless something of shattering consequence happened to alter his viewpoint, he would not again contemplate an attempted escape that left old man Quinn and Mary-Ann in greater danger on account of his actions.

'All right, Greg,' Thorne announced after waiting and watching patiently for the mounted trooper to hitch the lead line around his saddlehorn. 'You know what you have to do so there's no point in us going over it again?'

'Right, Merle. I'll see all you guys, uh?'

He raised a hand and grinned down at those close to him and the Apache who still squatted against the wall beside the way station doorway. But the patches of high colour and the vicious glint showed on his cheeks and in his eyes as his glance raked over the shattered window and he saw Sergeant Delany spit a stream of saliva out onto the thirsty ground.

'On your way, Greg!' Thorne ordered as he saw the trooper's reaction to the non-com's tacit contempt.

Priest heeled his horse into motion and the one behind him moved in unison. Then the trooper kept moving at the same easy pace as he half turned in the saddle to glare back at the broken window and taunt: 'Keep gettin' madder at me, Delany! Time I get back, you'll maybe be ready to spit blood, uh?'

Then he demanded a canter of the two horses under his control and began to raise an elongated cloud of dust in back of him. Which was quick to settle in the parched, still air after he was gone. But remained in sight at the centre of the widening canyon to the south long after the thud of hooves were muted by distance. Before this had happened, Ehrman laughed at the grim-faced Delany and growled:

'So the worm turns, Sarge?'

'Seems to me, Trooper, you're both low enough to the ground to be the same breed as that creature!' the non-com rasped.

'But they're not wriggling on the hook as bait for a big fish, soldier!' Merle Thorne growled with a sneer and acted to defuse Ehrman's anger and trigger another harsh laugh from him.

Charlie Smiles vented a similar sound of enjoyment and yelled: 'Hey, that's pretty damn good, uh dude? You enjoy the joke like me, I reckon?'

'Sometimes, feller,' the Virginian answered evenly as he moved as close as he could to the window without pushing his face between the ugly shards. 'But when I'm caught I look at things from a different angle.'

SEVEN

FOR A time after the beat of hooves had faded from earshot and all the ambushers save for the Apache had gone around to the rear of the way station – where they were heard to enter the living quarters of the place – there was a speechless silence in the crowded public room. Which persisted after Delany had moved to join Rivers and Wade on the bench to one side and Zucconi backed away to lower himself on to one of the armchairs, leaving Adam Steele standing at the window – peering out over a restricted panorama of the canyon's southern length. And still peering even after the two horses with just one living rider and the dust cloud they raised had disappeared from his range of vision.

'He won't be able to ride that fast for very long, Steele,' Delany said.

'Not in this heat,' the Virginian agreed.

'North Bend spread is close to fifteen miles from here, I'd say. To the house.'

'Grateful to you.'

'Be awhile before that turncoat deserter gets there.'

'And from what I've heard about Mr Cornelius Attwood,' the short and skinny, blonde-headed Corporal Rivers put in dully as he stared into the middle distance, 'there ain't no telling what'll happen when he hears about this.'

Steele turned away from the shattered window and his stoical survey of the terrain which lay to the south. Which was, of course, no different to when he had first seen it from the top of the rise before the fusillade of killing gunshots had concentrated his attention on the way station. On this side of the canyon's narrow point the rock walls widened out at much the same rate as to the north. But the height of the flanking cliffs gradually reduced so that, instead of ending at a mouth, the southern section became no more than a broad valley between low, rocky hills after the walls gave way to slopes. Afternoon heat shimmer was as opaquely close as that of midday, and to its veiling barrier Steele could see that the floor of the canyon and the bottom land of the valley beyond were almost as barren as the rock walls and the scree- and boulder-strewn slopes. Just ground-hugging brush and an infrequent fat Cholla or spider-legged Ocotillo that reached a few feet higher into the aridly heated air broke the dust-powdered monotony of the land to either side of the arrow-straight trail.

It was not the kind of terrain over which one prisoner, let alone a whole bunch of them, stood much chance of making a surreptitious escape.

'Man that sets any store by rumours is an out-and-out fool, Corporal!' Delany snapped.

The bushy-moustached, powerfully-built Wade who had nodded his agreement with what Rivers said now shook his head to deny the sergeant's contention. And spread a mournful expression across his youthful face, to match his tone of voice when he said: 'I ain't never heard a good word spoke of that man. And I always say there ain't no stink of shit without shit.'

Mary-Ann Slattery vented a choked gasp.

'Watch your language in the presence of a lady, soldier!' Quinn growled, and curled a protective arm around the woman's narrow shoulders.

'Nothin' either of you said did a thing to help out the situation!' Delany censured, glowering at the contrite Wade and the unrepentant Rivers.

'Beg pardon, ma'am,' the trooper offered, touching his cap. 'Unused to being in the company of ladies. Just didn't think.'

'Please don't worry about it,' the woman assured, and even managed to raise a faint smile that she shared between the young trooper and the old-timer as she rose to her feet. 'It is the meaning of what you say rather than the way in which you express yourself that disturbs me. And the fact that Count Zucconi, who is a friend of Cornelius Attwood, does not feel able to contradict you?'

Steele looked hard at Mary-Ann, concerned that she was

suddenly too self-controlled as she shifted her quizzical gaze about the room and spoke in a conversational tone. But he saw no sign that it was a charade she was performing to conceal or to guard against the threat of a hysterical outburst.

The Italian, who became the final focal point of her inquisitive gaze, made to rise from his chair. Then the expression of defensiveness that suggested he was about to take issue with what had been said was replaced by a look of resignation. And he eased back into the chair and contented his sense of propriety with a tip of his hat. Before he replied:

'I cannot deny, *signora*, that I know Mr Attwood to be a man of volatile temperament. A man does not become so rich and so powerful as he by being soft-hearted and surrendering without a struggle to the attacks of enemies. He is a man easy to anger and one I would not care to cross the swords with when he is angered. He is sure to be very angry indeed when he learns that these outlaws are holding me for ransom.'

'We're not outlaws, mister!' the Apache countered harshly as he stepped in front of the window. 'We're cowpunchers who are owed by that Attwood sonofabitch! You two guys drag your asses back from here!'

The Indian brave looked close to the brink of a killing rage – his dark eyes ablaze and a tic working spasmodically across his right, sucked-in cheek. He shared the powerful emotion equally among everyone in the room as he made his rebuttal to the accusation of being an outlaw. But then confined it to Steele and Zucconi as he thrust his rifle barrel between the dangerous shards of glass in the window frame and swung it with his gaze back and forth between the two prisoners who were closest to him.

'Greg and Frank, too, before they enlisted, they were — '

The Virginian waited for the Italian to make the first move. And, like the Apache, did not expect the man to respond aggressively.

Zucconi began to rise from the chair, half turned toward Charlie Smiles, seemingly as stunned as everyone else by the abruptness and violence of the Indian's intrusion. And then the muzzle of the Winchester and the blazing eyes started to track away from him.

For the stretched seconds since the young brave had announced his presence at the window, Steele had remained in a half turn toward him: an expression of mild surprise fixed to his face. Now he powered into a faster part-turn and leaned forward as he raised both his gloved hands from his sides. This as the look of surprise was displaced by a killer's grin of intent to finish what he had started.

Smiles saw the sudden move and attempted to jerk the rifle back out of the window, his anger becoming pleasure as he relished the prospect of outwitting the white-eyes again: perhaps killing him for his reckless audacity. But the Apache's sense of well being was short-lived. For the Virginian's arms moved in a blur of speed to give him a two-handed grip on the rifle at the moment Smiles started to withdraw it – the right palm upwards at the muzzle and the left palm down at the frame.

Alarm tinged the fresh anger that showed on the brave's face now, as a sound between a grunt and a snarl was vented through his gritted teeth. And he tried to swing the rifle to aim at Steele as his attempt to withdraw it was halted.

The woman squealed with a mixture of surprise and pain as Quinn lunged off the bench with a curse, to curl an arm around her and take her hard to the floor with him. Rivers and Wade snarled profanities, too. But were silenced and spurred into movement by a snapped command from Delany – the sergeant powering toward the Italian, clawed hands reaching to fasten on the man and drag him to the floor.

Steele was aware of the sounds and scurrying movements at his back only on the periphery of his consciousness. Was not certain if he yet heard other voices in other rooms of the way station or whether he simply imagined them.

The Apache had possessed the self-control to hold back from squeezing the trigger of the rifle for this long. Now, as Steele forced his right hand up and his left down, the brave's forefinger was levered into a firing action. And a bullet cracked from the Winchester's canted barrel to smash deep into a ceiling beam.

Now there was no doubt in the Virginian's mind that the men in the rear of the building were yelling in response to the unseen disturbance at the front. But he continued to discount all other considerations while he pressed home his attack on Charlie Smiles – switched his pulling action against the rifle into a pushing one. Caught the Apache off-balance and so needed little brute force to send him stumbling into an awkward, back-stepping gait. Used all the strength at his command, though, to power a dive through the window frame while he kept a tenacious hold on the rifle.

A second gunshot sounded within the tension-filled room, which was still permeated by the acrid taint of black powder smoke from the first. Somebody made a gasping sound and Thorne shrieked:

'Everyone freeze, you bastards!'

Then Steele was out of the window, heard clearly the tinkle of breaking glass as the shards he had displaced from the frame fell to the ground. Felt the warmth of blood on his left thigh where one needle-pointed fragment had cut him before it was removed. A moment later his awareness was once again totally confined to himself in relation to the Indian: as the Apache relinquished his hold on the Winchester – and whipped his curled right hand toward his holstered revolver. Smiles was starting to fall over backwards then and his instinct should have been to try to break the fall. Instead, he attempted an eye gouging attack with his left hand. Steele refused to be distracted by the move, but was not able to restrain a groan of pain as his knees and feet crashed to the ground. Then experienced a fleeting glow of satisfaction when the Apache screamed to a much higher pitch – giving vocal release to the searing agony he felt a moment later when the stock of the rifle was smashed into his crotch.

Now the brave was a victim of involuntary instinct – clawed both his hands to the source of his pain as he ducked his head, brought his knees up to his chest and rolled onto his side. Quieter now, as he fought to renew the breath expended by the scream.

The Virginian's every instinct during the next few moments of nerve-rending time was concerned with self-preservation. And thus was he able to ignore the pains of the jarring impact with the rock hard ground – and maybe even to rise above what in other circumstances would have been the disabling effects of the fall – for as long as it took to get the Indian's life on the line.

First he pumped the lever action of the repeater as he withdrew it from the rolling-over form of the gasping Indian. Next used it as a crutch to help him fast to his feet. Submitted to the illogical need to concentrate his blurred gaze on the expended shell which lay glinting in the dust until he was fully erect. Finally took one staggering step, pushed the muzzle of the rifle into the gaping mouth of Charlie Smiles and turned to peer at the window of the way station's public room at the same moment he gave a jerk of the Winchester to wrench the brave's head into a half turn.

'Hold it!' a man roared.

'The Apache's holding his own, feller,' Steele answered through gritted teeth. 'Do what I can to keep a grip on myself.'

EIGHT

CHARLIE SMILES kept swallowing hard and this was transmitted outwardly as a sucking motion and sound against the evil-tasting metal of the recently-fired rifle with its muzzle jammed hard to the back of his throat.

The same man who had yelled the command out of the way station window now spoke with less strident urgency. 'The trooper's dead, dude. Doc's inclined to shoot first and think about it later — '

'Aw, shit, I — '

'Make less with the mouth, Doc. Dude, nobody else has to get blasted. Unless you kill Charlie.'

Steele had recognized the voice of Merle Thorne while his vision was still blurred by pain that made it seem he was standing in a raging fire with searing flames leaping up about his legs. Then, as he concentrated as intently on the area from which the voice came as he had on the ejected shellcase in the dust moments ago, the scene came starkly into focus – the element-bleached facade of the building with the dark wooden door flanked by two windows, one glinting in the bright sunlight of mid-afternoon and the other glassless. At the broken window the broad torso and scowling face of the man who had a far greater regard for his Apache partner than for the rest of the men who had helped him with the ambush.

This degree of liking by Thorne for Smiles was what had tipped the balance in the Virginian's mind to launch him into the desperate action. But the fact that he had judged the situation right and succeeded this far did not spark any sense of satisfaction as he locked eyes with the man who aimed an Army Colt at him out the window. For the high tension of anger and fear and hatred and greed and an erratically burning fuse of badly injured pride was an unstable, near-palpable presence in the hot, dry air.

'They have your friends at gunpoint, sir!' Zucconi called from the dark sun-shaded room in back of Thorne.

'He's right, Sergeant,' Corporal Rivers reported miserably. 'Eddie Wade is dead for sure.'

Frank Ehrman growled spitefully: 'I never could abide that guy's long face at the post and — '

'Less mouth, all of you!' Thorne shrieked, the pitch of his voice more revealing of the degree of his anger than was his unflinching expression of hostility, as his eyes remained in a fixed stare on Steele's face and the revolver and his hand fisted around it were as steady as fused rock. Stretched seconds of utter silence slid into history while Thorne fought to control his anger to an extent that would allow him to speak in a normal tone. Then, as the suffering Apache ended the brittle stillness with a sucking gulp, the man at the window said to the Virginian: 'Attwood's buddy told it like it is, dude. Charlie gets it, they get it and you get it. The two soldier boys as well, maybe. We still have Zucconi who was the only guy we ever wanted anyways.'

'I wish for no one else to be killed on my account!' the Italian pleaded.

'Merle said to be quiet!' Harding snapped.

Steele, salty runnels among the bristles on his lower face and with more sweat pasting his clothes to his skin, welcomed the pause during which he was able to catch his breath and secretly indulge his pains: as, forcing himself to ignore every other aspect of the dangerous situation, he constantly watched Thorne while he kept the Apache in view on the lower periphery of his vision. Now he said: 'Seems we have the making of a deal, feller?'

'Spit it out, dude.'

'You keep Zucconi and turn the rest of us loose.'

In back of the immobile and stone-faced Thorne, Delany rasped: 'Bastard!'

The Italian added, with satisfaction: '*Buono.*'

Thorne expressed brief vexation with the interruptions, then asked in an even tone: 'Just to turn you loose ain't enough, would be my guess?'

'My horse and rifle. Quinn's wagon and team. The mounts of the sergeant and — '

'Rivers and me ain't leavin' — '

There was a brief flurry of sound and movement in the room that caused the non-com to curtail his protest. Thorne's eyes suddenly expressed a plea toward Steele and then the disturbance was ended by a thud, a gasp of forcefully expelled air and a louder thump.

'Knocked him out is all, Merle!' Frank Ehrman reported with a tone akin to glee.

'His head's bleeding,' Mary-Ann Slattery said, shocked.

'It's all right, ma'am, he's breathin' fine,' Rivers assured her.

The tacit entreaty for the Virginian not to react impulsively to the spontaneous violence triggered by a third party was abruptly gone from Thorne's features. And maybe for an instant he expressed relief – even gratitude. But then he looked his usual hard self as he asked sardonically against a renewed bout of gulping by the Apache: 'You want Charlie to go along with you to wipe your asses after you taken a crap, and for the rest of us to whistle *Dixie* while you ride into the settin' friggin' sun, dude?'

'Charlie Smiles isn't smiling at that joke, feller,' Steele said evenly, and pushed the Winchester muzzle harder against the back of the Apache's throat.

It drew a dry retching sound from the hapless brave and Thorne grimaced, like he was feeling the same kind of pain as the Indian, who continued to clutch at his punished groin. Then:

'All right, all right! Let him up and I'll — '

'He gets up when the wagon and horses and my rifle and you and everybody else are out here, feller,' the Virginian cut in, aware that the interruption brought Thorne again close to the danger point of explosive anger.

'You got a death wish or somethin', mister?' Harding growled.

'I've got as much to live for as anyone else around here, I reckon. And as much chance of dying for nothing.'

'All right, all right!' Thorne snapped. 'Frank, take the corporal and the old man out back and have them fix up the wagon for rollin' and the three horses for ridin'. And bring the dude's fancy rifle with you when everythin' else is done.'

'You're the boss, Merle,' the scar-faced trooper acknowledged in a grudging tone that expressed his dissatisfaction with what was happening.

'That I friggin' am!' Thorne snarled for the benefit of everyone, after three pairs of footfalls sounded in the room behind him. 'And I'm doin' what I have to do to keep one of my boys from gettin' his head blown off! But ain't just Charlie got his ass on the line here! One wrong move and we got us a friggin' bloodbath that'll go down in friggin' history! Move or sound! So let's all of us keep real quiet, all right!'

Thorne's imperious edict was obeyed to the best of everyone's ability. Some people found themselves breathing with more ragged noise than was usual, the woman was unable to check a stifled sob from time to time, the Apache continued to vent the involuntary gulping sounds and out at the stable and in the corral at the rear of the way station, Ehrman and Rivers and Amos Quinn seemed to do as much as they could to labour quietly at their appointed tasks.

Tension stretched the measurement of time. The stench of the decomposing corpses in the well suddenly became very evident. But then Steele got to be more aware of the stink of his own sweat-run body. He felt the individual points of pain at each knee and in each shin – even where his leg had been gashed by the glass. He foresaw the danger of overconcentration on the gunman at the window leading to a blurring of his vision again and so switched his attention fleetingly elsewhere at irregular intervals. And was able to judge from the movement of the shadow of a corner of the way station that the men out back of the place did not take an inordinate length of time to do what was asked of them. Ten minutes, more or less, between Merle Thorne's threat of wholesale slaughter and the halting of the wagon and three saddled horses on the trail to the south of the way station's facade. Old man Quinn leading his team by a bridle, the short and skinny cavalry corporal holding the other horses by the reins and the ugly Frank Ehrman covering both with a rifle in each hand – one of these weapons the Colt Hartford.

'Let Charlie up now, Steele,' Thorne instructed after hooves had ceased to clop and wheels to creak.

'Everyone outside, feller.'

'Doc, Luther, leave your guns in here and haul that sergeant out front.'

'Hell, Merle — '

'I don't like — '

'You, Zucconi,' Thorne cut in on both his men's complaints. 'Come on over here.'

'*Si.*'

The tall, slim, good-looking Italian aristocrat appeared at the window beside Thorne. His hair and teeth did not seem to be so white now, since his skin was pale under the dark of race and tan. Fear gave him a gaunt and sickly appearance that aged him. His blue eyes, no longer so clear, gazed into the middle distance with an odd expression that seemed at one and the same time to convey condemnation and thanksgiving toward whatever image he elected to conjure up against the backdrop of reality out there in the harsh sunlight. When Thorne shifted the Colt and pressed the muzzle to the man's neck just below the left ear, the Italian stiffened and remained in a state of ramrod rigidity. But otherwise did not alter his serene attitude.

'Frank, ditch your guns and back off from them,' Thorne instructed as the way station door folded open. 'Lady, you go outside with the others. Steele, that's as far as I'm willin' to go. So you better move away from Charlie, get your fancy gun and get yourself and your people outta here. You don't do that, startin' right now, we reached a real dead end.'

While he spoke, the grim-faced Luther Schuler and the scowling Doc Harding emerged from the doorway, each dragging the unconscious Delany by a wrist. Following his orders more resentfully than the two civilians, Frank Ehrman waited until the wan faced Mary-Ann had moved on unsteady legs over the threshold from the way station before he stooped to place the Winchester and Colt Hartford rifles on the ground. He stayed on his haunches, his hatred for the world in general and Adam Steele in particular gradually expanding as he unfastened his holster flap and withdrew the Army Colt revolver. For perhaps as long as two seconds he was obviously struggling against a near overwhelming compulsion to explode a volley of shots toward the Virginian, who was not in a position to see this. But Rivers rasped:

'Don't be crazy, Trooper!'

For a split second more, the unassuming cavalry corporal became the sole object of the squatting man's vicious animosity. But then Ehrman allowed the revolver to slip from his grasp and spread a grin of pure pleasure across his broken-nosed, scar-tissue-marred face as he unfolded to his full height. When he allowed:

'Okay, Corporal. Fittin' the last order I ever obeyed in the lousy friggin' army came from the kinda lousy friggin' half-assed sonofabitch that I always hated worse and — '

'There you go, feller,' Steele cut in evenly on the trooper's diatribe, and eased the rifle muzzle gently out of the Apache's mouth before he sidestepped away from the man. For the first time since he made the brave his prisoner in such a brutal way, he took a two-handed grip on the repeater. And he kept it aimed at the Indian who sat up nd began to rasp a stream of obscenities in the American, Mexican and Apache languages between spitting out globules of saliva.

'Charlie, don't lose your head now I saved it for you!' Thorne snapped.

'Corporal, go get your sergeant,' Steele instructed as he continued to move toward the saddle horses in the wake of the Apache's tirade.

'Yessir.'

'Come on over here, Mrs Slattery,' Amos Quinn called croakily.

'Shit, Merle,' Doc Harding complained, and his fat, grey-fleshed face looked to be childishly close to tears as his tiny eyes in their red rims watched the slender form of the woman go toward the chattel-laden wagon.

'All of us out here could get our friggin' heads shot off, Merle!' the Indian-hating Schuler growled bitterly, his pockmarked face a mask of resentment that was directed at everyone, friend and foe alike.

'I owe you, white eyes,' Charlie Smiles said, in control of himself now as he remained seated on the ground. And as he began the threat, he very carefully eased the Colt from its holster and his knife from its sheath, gripping the butt and the hilt between the thumb and forefinger of each hand. 'But our business is with somebody else right now. Once before, I get close enough to reach out and touch you before you know I am with you. There will be another time and place for this to happen. When it will be my pleasure to repay the debt of pain and shame I owe you.'

The Apache tossed the knife in one direction and the revolver in another. Then began to rise painfully to his feet as Luther Schuler murmured:

'Stupid Injun bastard!'

Amos Quinn helped the woman to climb up onto the seat of the wagon and then hastily clambered aboard after her while Rivers inched tentatively to where Delany was sprawled and then dragged the senior non-com with ungentle speed back to where the horses waited.

Outwardly mistrustful of the passiveness of the hard-eyed men who watched him, but behind this veneer experiencing a sense of satisfaction that this gamble on the reading of Merle Thorne's character had paid off, the Virginian carefully exchanged the Apache's Winchester for his own rifle. And made no offer of help to Rivers as the young soldier struggled to slump the limp weight of the stockily-built Delany across a saddle.

Quinn leaned to the side to look back along his wagon and call: 'Ready to pull out, young feller?'

'Reckon so.'

Rivers was not inclined to make the unconscious, bloody-templed Delany fast to the saddle. Instead, elected to ride alongside the sergeant's mount, holding both sets of reins in one hand while with the other he kept the senseless man from falling by pressing down on the small of his back.

During these final preliminaries to the departure, Steele stood with one hand on the horn of his saddle: his other hand fisted around the uncocked rifle canted to his right shoulder, gloved thumb against the hammer. Then, as Quinn set the rig rolling and Rivers started the two army horses, the Virginian swung up astride his black stallion. He could not prevent his face showing the grimace of pain that the action caused to streak along both legs. And the hot air that was forced out through his clenched teeth made a whistling sound.

'You will hurt much more after our next meeting, white eyes!' Charlie Smiles called as he stood, not yet at his full height, watching Steele ride away down the southern section of the canyon.

Half-turned from the waist so that he was able to keep all the men out front of the way station under surveillance, the Virginian drawled: 'Move any closer to those guns, Trooper, and next hurt you feel will be your last.'

Frank Ehrman halted as if turned to rock. But held that attitude for just a moment. Before he turned his head and from the scowling curl of his lips directed a stream of saliva toward but far short of Steele.

'Luther, Doc, get in here and haul the corpse outside!' Merle Thorne ordered. 'Frank, come take a turn watchin' the prisoner! Charlie, you get in the back and rest up awhile!'

The men moved with resentful lethargy to comply with the commands as the wagon and its trailing riders made slow progress in lengthening the distance from the way station.

Then, after the cavalry trooper and the Apache had gone into the building, Harding and Schuler re-emerged – dragging the corpse of Eddie Wade in the same manner they had hauled the unconscious Delany outside. Merle Thorne came out after them to stand and gaze fixedly after the escapers. He had evidently already given instructions on the disposal of the fresh corpse, for the uniform-clad figure was taken to the well, raised on to the wall and tipped over it.

'He died doin' his duty, that's for sure,' Rivers said in a melancholic tone as he faced front again after watching the undignified dumping of the trooper's remains. 'Took a bullet meant for that foreign buddy of Attwood.'

Steele pushed the Colt Hartford forcefully into the forward-slung boot as he turned from watching Harding and Schuler ambling away from the well. Drawled: 'Another fighter who didn't go the distance, feller.'

'Sir?'

'Wade and the Captain both. Went out for the Count.'

NINE

THEY WERE less than a mile down the trail from the way station when Sergeant Delany came violently back to consciousness. He uttered a deep-throated cry of pain that surprised the tense corporal who rode alongside him – and Rivers instinctively snatched his hand away from the rousing man instead of strengthening his hold on him. So that when Delany's stocky frame involuntarily spasmed in the wake of his vocal reaction to agony, the sergeant slid off the smoothness of the saddle and dropped head first to the ground: too disorientated to even try to break the fall. He cried out again, and snarled an obscenity, as the previously broken skin under a crust of congealed blood on his right temple was reopened. And fresh deep crimson began to flow, dulling by contrast the auburn of his hair, as he sprawled out in a spreadeagled attitude on the trail – eyes tightly closed, teeth clenched between curled-back lips and every muscle in his body knotted. Like he expected to be the victim of some other form of punishing effect.

Steele and Rivers had both been looking back toward the way station and the trio of men who stood out front of it, diminishing in perspective, when Delany yelled and jolted out of senselessness. And both spontaneously reined in their horses. Quinn was just a moment later in bringing the wagon to a sudden halt after he leaned out to look back past the load to see what had happened.

'What was that?' the woman demanded, her voice edged with fear.

'Easy, Mary-Ann,' old man Quinn replied placatingly. 'The soldier just come out of it.'

But the fresh jolt to her insecure composure had been too great and she broke down into a fit of weeping. And Quinn remained aboard the wagon to comfort her. While the anxious Rivers swung awkwardly out of his saddle and crouched beside Delany. His voice a rasping whisper from the shock as he mixed up questions with explanations in his eagerness to know that the sergeant was not so badly hurt as the amount of spilled blood suggested, and would be able to reassume command of the much reduced army presence. This as the Virginian stayed astride his mount and divided his attention between the distant way station and the two uniformed men below him – had the satisfaction of seeing Thorne, Harding and Schuler go from sight into the building: and then felt the need to conceal his chagrin when he glanced down at the blood-run face of the spreadeagled Delany and saw the man was staring back up at him with a mixture of anger and disgust behind the pain.

'You're a crazy mad sonofabitch that could have got every one of us killed, mister!' the sergeant said, spitting out the condemnation with more venom than his hurt would allow him to show on his square-featured, element-scarred face. Only his lips, eyelids and Adam's apple moved while his torso and limbs remained as inert as those of a dead man.

Rivers, whose rapid-fire stream of talk had been interrupted in full flood, showed a wide grin of relief and rocked back on his heels as the sergeant revealed he was mentally stable. Then the surge of euphoria was gone as he realized Delany could seemingly not move and was still bleeding steadily, and consternation formed his expression again as he blurted:

'Sergeant, we're gonna have to do somethin' about your wound! And I reckon it'll be best if you ride aboard the — '

'Trooper Wade's as dead as the captain, right?' Delany rasped, shifting his gaze from the impassive Steele to the anxious Rivers. Then he raked his eyes across their narrowed sockets to glimpse on the periphery of his vision the distant way station which now had a smudge of woodsmoke showing above the chimney at the rear. 'And the bigwig foreigner is still a prisoner of Frank Ehrman and the others back there?'

He pointedly avoided looking at the Virginian as he returned his inquiring gaze to the corporal. Could not fail to be aware of the wagon, but elected to ignore it as Rivers nodded vigorously and waited eagerly to repeat those sections of his hastily-delivered report that Delany had apparently failed to assimilate.

'That's right, Sarge. But the lady and the other civilian got away free and clear as well and — '

'If Steele and his friends ever were our responsibility, Corporal, they sure as hell ain't no more!' the injured man said with grim determination, and chanced moving one hand to his head. He showed a grimace of distaste, that seemed somehow more deeply felt than the earlier expression of pain, after he shifted his hand away from the wound and saw the blood on the fingers. 'Be obliged now, if you'd give me a hand to get on my mount.'

'But, Sarge — '

The skinny, short-statured younger non-com eyed the blood-stained hand extended toward him with unconcealed aversion. Then snapped his head one way and another – conveying a tacit plea for backing from Steele and the woman and old-timer who were now down off the wagon.

'He's your boss, feller,' the Virginian pointed out with an almost imperceptible shrug of his shoulders.

'Damn right, Corporal!' Delany snarled, and made an unsuccessful attempt to struggle up into a sitting attitude. But he got the back of his head and one shoulder just an inch or so off the ground before he was forced to give in to the dictates of his punished system. Then rasped before Rivers could start a new protest: 'And I'm givin' the orders you're either gonna obey or face the consequences of refusin' to obey.'

Mary-Ann Slattery, dry-eyed now but looking sick still from the effects of the continuing ordeal, was able to overcome her own distress in the presence of somebody she considered in a worse state than herself. And she pulled free of Amos Quinn's supporting grasp of her and hurried away from the wagon.

'That's nonsense!' she blurted forcefully and her expression of entreaty was a match for that on the youthful face of Rivers when she looked up at the mounted Virginian to demand: 'Tell him it's nonsense, Mr Steele?'

'Ma'am, I'll thank you to . . .' Delany began, still fighting to regain his breath after the exertion of a few moments ago.

'It's army regulations,' Steele said when the non-com's exhaustion caused him to curtail what he was saying. 'But those kind of rules are the same as all the others.'

'Made to be broke, uh young feller?' the gangling, near-toothless, grey-haired old man said hurriedly as he continued to cast anxious glances back up the trail. To where the way station would have had an abandoned appearance had it not been for the thicker column of smoke that rose from its chimney to be quickly disintegrated by the hot air currents roiling between the canyon walls.

'Corporal, you'll face court martial for dereliction of duty while actively engaged on a mission of — '

Rivers abruptly rose to his feet and with an effort of will spread a determined expression across his immature face. The senior non-com had needed to screw his eyes tightly closed while he gathered strength to snarl the threat of military retribution at the wavering corporal. Now sensed the shadow of the standing man fall across his face and cut short what he was saying as he snapped open his eyes.

'Sorry, Sergeant Delany, but I'm assumin' command,' Rivers announced, his voice pitched far short of a shout, but its tone strong with unfamiliar authority. He stood almost to attention as he gazed fixedly toward the way station but probably did not see it. He kept clenching and unclenching his fists where they hung at his sides. 'On the grounds that you can't do it on account of bein' too badly wounded. Willin' to stand court martial if I have to.'

'Ain't no if about it, you crazy — ' the sergeant started, his amazement at this turn of events robbing him of the ability to look or sound as menacing as he felt.

'Be glad to be a witness that you done the right thing, son,' Amos Quinn assured.

'Me, too, young man,' Mary-Ann Slattery added. 'But now I think — '

'Grateful to you both,' Rivers cut in, after tentatively letting go of the middle distance world in which he had been safely detached while he made his opening bid for power. And now it was clear to see that he was experiencing something akin to pride in achievement as he surveyed everything and everybody in his surroundings with a cool, appraising gaze. 'But we got to get first things done first. Everythin's quiet back there where they got Mr Zucconi right now. But no tellin' what that Thorne guy and the rest are hatchin' up inside the place. Best we get far as we can away from here while the light of day is with us. Quick as we can, too. So we can have the sergeant tended to. Grateful if you'll allow him to ride aboard the wagon, Mr Quinn. If that don't leave no room for you, ma'am, you willin' and able to ride the sergeant's horse?'

'Long as he can ride sittin' up on the seat, son,' the old-timer agreed eagerly after a rueful glance at the heavily and untidily laden wagon. 'Don't hardly know where to begin takin' off stuff so the whole kit and caboodle don't come tumblin' down.'

'That's all right, sir. We have to do the best that we can in the circumstances. Ma'am?'

'I can ride the horse, Corporal,' Mary-Ann assured Rivers absently while she watched Delany with a concerned frown – having seen how the blood had kept on oozing from the gash at the side of his head and how the injured man's will to take issue with what was happening had gradually diminished to a point where he appeared utterly submissive. 'But it seems to me we have to give some attention to your sergeant's injury before we start. Or he could bleed to death.'

She lowered her voice to a rasping whisper as she concluded her opinion, but from the brink of delirium Delany heard what she said and vented a gleeful laugh. Then challenged:

'No friggin' chance, lady. When all my blood's gone I'll live on the piss in my bladder if I have to. Long as it's needed for me to see Chuck Rivers gets what he has comin' to him.'

'He's sick, ma'am, or else he wouldn't use that kinda language in front — '

'Bandage him up and get him loaded on the wagon,' Steele cut in on the corporal's embarrassed apology, his tone carrying the same degree of impatience as was seen in his coal-black eyes. 'Or stand around here making Sunday-after-meeting small talk without me.'

'Didn't hear any small talk about asking you to stay, Mr Steele?' the woman suggested caustically.

'Hey now, Mary-Ann, he done good for us and we still need — ' the old man insisted anxiously.

'Sir, I was goin' to request the loan of your rifle,' Rivers said, just as anxiously. 'And assumed you'd be willin' to escort your friends to a place of safety at the North Bend Ranch of Mr Attwood. While I remained in this area to maintain a watch on the place where Mr Zucconi is bein' held prisoner, sir.' The young corporal's nervousness increased as he found his gaze caught in the steady, suddenly impassive trap of the Virginian's unblinking stare. And his voice became gradually more unnaturally formal. But then he assumed the stance to attention and firmed his expression and his tone as he finished: 'Since you have the only firearm, sir, unless you are prepared to loan it to me willingly, I feel it is my duty to commandeer it. Beggin' your pardon, sir.'

'Trooper,' Steele said softly, and Rivers was encouraged by the seeming friendliness of the tone to adopt a less rigid and more informal attitude.

'Sir?' And now appeared more youthful and almost flimsily thin as he looked at, rather than toward Adam Steele – and saw the latent brutality that gleamed from just beneath the surface of the mirthless grin fixed to the sweat-run, dirt-streaked, heavily grey-stubbled face.

'You should know: that if it ever happens you have this rifle and I don't, you best be careful if you feel the need to scratch your rear.'

The disconcerted corporal was too mesmerized by the power of the Virginian's expression to fully comprehend what was being said to him. He swallowed hard and queried: 'Yes?'

'Don't scratch your ass, young feller, on account of there'll be a rifle stuck up it,' Amos Quinn explained, and gestured to the woman that she should begin to carry out the first part of the suggestion Steele had made about tending to the injured sergeant.

'And seein' the kind of no-account soldier you've turned out to be,' Delany growled acidly through gritted teeth and with his eyes still tightly closed, 'I figure a shot up your asshole will likely blow your brains out.'

Rivers wrenched his head around to look in turn at the old-timer and the sergeant as each man made his unhelpful comment. Then he directed his gaze of expanding desperation toward Mary-Ann Slattery, but the woman was engrossed in making bandages from a piece of fabric she had taken off the wagon.

'The hell with all of you!' he rasped through a grimace. 'I know I ain't the best friggin' soldier in the United States Army, but I know how to do my duty. You people do like I told you. I'll stay on watch here, without no weapon if that's the way it has to be. And I'll thank you to inform Mr Attwood that I'm here and I'll be able to give him a full report on the enemy's — '

'Sounds good, young feller,' Quinn cut in from where he squatted, holding up the head of the grimacing but uncomplaining Delany so that Mary-Ann was able to bandage the wound after cleaning off the old blood. 'That sounds real good to me. A soldier has to do his duty, best he can when there ain't no higher ranker to tell him what to do. And way things have shaped up around here, seems to me you settled on the right thing to do. In the circumstances, like.'

While Rivers listened, grim-faced, and maintained an unblinking watch on the way station up the trail, the old-timer shared an imploring look among the busy woman, the almost unconscious sergeant and the Virginian, who now sat nonchalantly in the saddle, an impassive expression comfortably fixed on his face.

'That's the best I'm able to do,' Mary-Ann announced, still engrossed in tending to Delany as she half rose, surveyed her inexpert handiwork and then instructed: 'Right, Mr Quinn, Corporal . . . please help me to get him on the wagon?'

Carefully, with as much gentleness as they were able to manage, the young corporal and the old man followed the woman's directions in lifting Delany up off the trail and raising him onto the wagon seat. Where he was placed in an upright position and tied securely to the seat and an iron bedhead that was behind it. He groaned and sometimes rasped a curse, but his anger seemed to be directed at his own inability to conquer the disabling effects of his injury rather than at the three people helping him and the one watching. He was not coherent until he was safely held up on the seat by the ropes, and Rivers and Quinn had climbed down to the ground to check on the woman's opinion that nothing more could be done for the sergeant. Which was when he fought his chin up off his chest and then needed more physical effort to force the grudging words out of his throat:

'Damn you, Corporal, but it's like the civilian says. In the present situation, you're takin' the right course of action. God willin', I'll see to it Attwood knows . . .'

'I'm obliged to you, Sergeant,' Rivers put in as Delany's head sagged and his voice weakened from a whisper to incomprehensible raspings.

'Rest of us ready to leave now?' Steele asked as he halted his horse on the other side of the wagon from where the two men and the woman stood.

'Thought you'd already left,' Mary-Ann Slattery said with soft-toned venom. 'All the help you've been, you might just as well not have been here, seems to me.'

'Ma'am, like Mr Quinn already said, Steele got us clear this far,' Rivers reminded, as obdurate now as the Virginian, since Delany had spoken. 'And I'm chargin' him with your safety from here to North Bend?'

Looking up at the mounted man across the front of the form of the again-unconscious Delany, sagged against the ropes, the gaunt and pale young non-com expressed a tacit plea for moral support from the Virginian who until now had seemed bent on humiliating him.

'Second priority I had in mind when I made my play against the Apache, feller,' Steele said evenly. 'And nothing's changed.'

'I'm obliged to you, sir.' He threw up a hurried salute.

'Sure am glad we can get rollin' again,' Quinn said eagerly, and hurriedly climbed up on to the seat alongside the oblivious sergeant.

'Your first thought was to save your own neck!' Mary-Ann Slattery accused sardonically after she had allowed Rivers to escort her to where the horses waited at the rear of the wagon, and then to help her to mount Delany's gelding.

'Dead men are no help to anybody, lady,' the Virginian answered.

'Can't argue with that, that's for sure,' Quinn said, and looked back along the side of the wagon, beyond Steele, for an instruction to set the team horses moving.

'Except maybe to remind others of their own mortality,' Steele added.

'Move on out,' Rivers called, and tipped his hat rather than saluted to Mary-Ann, who gave him a curt nod and with pointed intent steered her horse to the opposite side of the wagon from where the Virginian rode.

A few moments later, when the wagon and its two flanking riders had settled into the measured cadence of an easy pace suitable for the still high heat of late afternoon, Amos Quinn leaned out to look back again at where the lone figure of Corporal Rivers stood beside his horse amid the settling dust of the departure. Then spat a globule of saliva on to a wheelrim and growled ruefully:

'Always said it – ain't hardly room to draw the thinnest of lines between bravery and stupidity.'

'It was his intention to be less foolhardy and brave with Adam Steele's rifle,' the woman reminded grimly.

'Didn't I tell him he could try to get it?' Steele asked across the backs of the team in the traces. 'But at least he wasn't so foolhardy as to wind up with it where I — '

'It's a crying pity my grandfather never knew your mother and father, Mr Steele,' Mary-Ann cut in acidly.

'Uh?' Amos Quinn grunted, disconcerted by the abrupt change of subject.

'He was a minister of religion and perhaps would have married them,' she added with a vitriolic sneer. 'Before they spawned you!'

'Hey now, Mary-Ann,' the old-timer blurted, snapping his head from side to side to show his pained expression to the scowling woman and the unprovoked man. 'I don't think we oughta forget we went through a whole lot of trouble that was our business before all this happened. And didn't have cause to call each other names and act like — '

'I'm just thankful I found out what kind of mean and selfish animal you are before I became . . .' She found herself unable to voice what she had obviously, until the ambush, considered might have been. And she stared fixedly ahead.

Torn between the secure future he had seen in the Virginian and what he hoped was the start of more than mere friendship with the woman, the old-timer's consternation increased by the moment. He seemed to give hurried consideration to a dozen different solutions while he pivoted his head from side to side. Then he settled on: 'Look, let's not any of us say anythin' else in haste until we ain't a part of all this no more? What d'you say?'

'I haven't yet said a word I don't consider anything short of the truth,' Mary-Ann Slattery responded with a disdainful sniff.

'Mr Steele?' Amos Quinn posed with a weary sigh after he realized he could expect nothing more forthcoming than this from her.

'At the right time, I'll be happy for anyone to have the last word, feller.'

The old-timer was fleetingly perplexed, but then shrugged his skinny shoulders and murmured with relief: 'Good.'

'That's just the half of it.'

'Uh?'

'Whole thing is goodbye.'

TEN

FOR AS long as backward glances from the slow-moving wagon saw the lone cavalryman as a part of the scene below the narrowest point of the canyon, the slighty-built Rivers remained standing on the centre of the trail beside his horse. Then he and everything in his immediate surroundings were swallowed up in the last vestige of the day's shimmering heat haze. And, as the desert night came with its usual speed across the short-lived evening, distance rather than the moonlit darkness placed the dutybound corporal out of sight.

A coyote howled, a bird screeched and a very far-off clap of thunder cracked. From elsewhere in the distance there came only the dull, monotonous thudding of silence to sound against the eardrums of the woman, the old-timer and the Virginian. From closer to hand there was just the familiar clop of hooves, jingle of harness, creak of timber and clatter of turning wheelrims. There was an illusion that these sounds were louder in the night than they had been in the brightness of day: but this was always so, even when tension of no kind rode with the travellers. But, without doubt, the events of the afternoon just gone and reflections upon what might happen in the immediate future had an amplifying effect on the sound of silence. To the extent where it seemed Mary-Ann and Quinn were afraid to interrupt it with mere words. While Steele appeared – or would have appeared to a stranger – as the most nervous of all: from the manner in which he constantly scanned the terrain on all sides.

Terrain that was now a vast and faintly undulating scrub desert encircled by low mountains at varying distances on every side. The canyon where the deadly ambush was sprung was now indistinguishable from the line of rugged, moon-shaped ridges to the north. These mountains were the closest for the first two hours of full, cold night: while those to the south gradually grew larger in perspective with every slow turn of the wagon wheels. And the high ground to the east and west of the arrow-straight trail across the meagrely-featured plain remained constantly many miles to the left and right. As the easy-paced trek progressed southward, the high ground ahead could be seen as less inhospitable than the country through which the wagon and its outriders passed. There was a quality of gentleness to it, generated by the lines of curves vastly outnumbering those of sharp angles – to suggest soft and perhaps lushly-vegetated hills with just an occasional grim-faced rock ridge or rearing outcrop. Maybe, too, there were creeks, or at least waterholes, in the hills where Cornelius Attwood's North Bend Ranch was sited.

Steele played host to this stray notion of fresh, sweet water as he tilted a canteen to his lips and sucked frugally at its time-tainted contents. And as he recorked the canteen acknowledged to himself that he might well be indulging in wishful thinking about the entire geology of the still-distant hills that were so steeped in moon-shadow to the south.

'Seein' you take that drink of water just reminds me of somethin', Mr Steele,' Amos Quinn said to break the long silence – that had previously only been broken by Mary-Ann Slattery, when from time to time she asked the old-timer to make the unfeeling soldier more comfortable behind the restraining ropes.

'You want some?' the Virginian responded absently, his mind still involved with a reverie of the kind of fine country that might lie down the trail.

'We want nothing from you, mister,' the woman snapped waspishly.

'You know we have plenty of our own, young feller,' the old man put in, and Steele emerged from the ruminative mood in time to see deep-set eyes in the heavily wrinkled face of Quinn shift their gaze from Mary-Ann to himself, the expression of condemnation altering fast to a look of mild rebuke. And he stemmed the rising note in his tone as he went on: 'Was gonna say, reminds me ain't none of us had a bite to eat since breakfast.

Which seems a lot longer ago than just this mornin'. But I got no feelin' of hunger.'

'Only person with no feelings at all could consider eating at a time like this!' she retorted icily. 'That man has been unconscious for too long. I'm sure he's dying.'

Steele was irritated with himself to find out how chill the night had become, and to see that both the woman and the old-timer had donned warm topcoats and mittens while he continued to ride through the moonlit darkness in the same manner as if the harsh sun were still blazing out of the sky. But it was not the fact of his unnecessary discomfort that irked him as he took the sheepskin coat off his bedroll and shrugged into it: instead, that he had allowed himself to become so detached from his immediate surroundings that he failed to notice such mundane details. And then he saw, too, after Quinn had directed another censorious glower at the woman, that they had also used blankets to drape warmly the inert form of the sergeant, slumped forward and head hung.

The degree of his self anger expanded as he realized the extent of the trance-like state into which he had so withdrawn from what was happening about him. And this ill-humour showed as a frown on his face, which Amos Quinn mistook as a sign of Steele's response to the woman's attitude.

'Shit!' the near toothless old-timer blurted, and had to struggle against losing a grip on his own temper. 'And I don't feel moved to say sorry for speakin' my mind no more, Mary-Ann Slattery! Same as I ain't gonna make no apologies for speakin' out against you like I done sometimes today, young feller!' He swung his head from one side to the other as he referred to each of the riders flanking him. Now peered directly ahead between the pair of easy-walking team horses as he went on: 'Can't be denied that not all of us was happy with the way things was this mornin'. And I guess there'd been some second thoughts about our plans even before this mornin'.'

'That was said before the trouble got started, old man,' Mary-Ann reminded with flint in her tone and ice in her eyes as she shot a glance across the front of the wagon at the again impassive Virginian.

'All right,' Quinn allowed, his own tone of voice softening. 'But we'd been doin' nothin' together for a long time except travellin' and seemin' not to get anyplace. Reckon it stands to reason we was gonna start to get on each other's nerves. Wonder of it was that it didn't happen sooner. But it didn't, and the longer we got along together without any of us ranklin' the other – or lettin' the others know we was rankled – the higher my hopes got for us we'd make out fine in the horse breedin' business.'

'It was never stated in words that *we'd* be in that business, old man,' the blonde with the unpretty but very alluring face said with pointed emphasis – and continued to peer fixedly down the trail like Quinn.

This while Steele maintained his all-around survey of the night-shrouded landscape: once again paying scant attention to his travelling companions as he instinctively sought for sources of potential danger. And his demeanour was a true reflection of his composed mood now. He was none the worse for having ridden for an unspecified length of time in a kind of self-induced stupor that left him without a single recollection of anything that happened while his mind was apparently a blank. And now he had come close enough to the rolling hills of the south to see that they were, indeed, lushly covered with grass. And that stands of timber and thickets of brush provided further evidence of water in the area. It looked nothing like Virginia, even in the flattering moonlight, but Virginia was in the past. In the future there was a piece of country, not unlike the sections he raked his gaze over now . . . maybe this very area of north eastern Arizona . . .

'But it was never *not* stated, Mary-Ann,' Quinn countered.

'That's right,' Steele admitted after several stretched seconds during which the widow woman and the old-timer thought he was back behind an impenetrable barrier of deep reflections again. 'Reckon I did more than my fair share of talking without ever saying what you wanted to hear?'

'Or didn't want to hear, young feller,' the old-timer said, melancholic. 'Until this mornin' before the trouble.' He needed to pause to give himself time to generate the surface signs of a change of mood. But it was apparent that the animated smile of excited eagerness he directed across at Steele was wafer thin, and brittle as a dry leaf. 'But what I started out to say just now . . . the trouble's changed things . . . you was ready to head off and go your own way . . . before we heard Thorne and them others kill them poor people at the stage-line way station? But since then you been lookin' out for us real good, Mr Steele. Helped us just like you done back in Barclay when Mary-Ann and me lost our loved ones. And I been thinking that a man . . . like you are . . . shit, a man that was all-fire set on cuttin' loose from folks he didn't want no more truck with . . . well, he wouldn't have seen out for us the way you have . . .'

It was as if the old-timer was reluctant to stop talking for fear that the Virginian was waiting for just such an interruption to douse the last flickering flames of his hopes. But the emotional strain he was under seemed abruptly to sap him physically, and he abandoned the pretence of faith in what he was saying as his narrow shoulders sagged and the false smile slipped from his emaciated face.

'Old man?' the woman asked, concerned that he might be sick in body as well as in spirit.

'Old fool Quinn is what I'll have to ask my friends to call me,' he growled, and again it was plain to see that it required a great effort of will for him to keep a tight control of himself. 'First for thinkin' that a young feller with ambition would have any use for a used-up has-been like me.' A harsh laugh that was not too far removed from a sob vented involuntarily from his throat before he concluded: 'And then I got to thinkin' things about you and me Mary-Ann that . . .'

He managed to trap within himself the sound that this time would surely have been a sob. And was then able to keep the wetness spilling from his eyes only by staring straight ahead and chewing on his slack lower lip.

During the first few seconds of the old-timer's latest efforts to keep a hold on his emotions, Mary-Ann Slattery glowered across at Steele – tacitly challenging him to do or say anything that would push Amos Quinn off the brink and into the humiliating well of self-pity. Then she accepted his initial non-response as a sign of intent, and concentrated her concerned attention on the old-timer.

Who, perhaps a full minute after he instituted the new silence, broke it with the assurance, spoken in a gratified tone:

'I'm okay now.'

The scrub desert had already begun to soften toward meadowland to either side of the lumbering wagon and unhurried riders: the grass patchy and parched among the scattered cacti, greasewoods, palo verde and mesquite trees. But the water that fed the lusher pastures of the hills reached out beneath the edge of the plain in only meagre quantities. Where the good, well-watered land began on the lower slopes of the first rises in the south, moonlight-glinting strands of barbed wire were tautly strung between four-feet-high posts.

Adam Steele saw the fences that enclosed vast tracts of land on both sides of the trail without the slightest stab of disappointment. The prospect of finding a piece of land for himself in these hills had served to reaffirm in his own mind the determination to locate and settle on just such a fine stretch of dirt, a comfortably long way from the nearest neighbour. So these sections were spoken for – it was a big country.

'You were there when I needed somebody to lean on, old man,' Mary-Ann murmured contritely. 'And if anything I said or did led you to believe I — '

'It's all right, Mary-Ann. Ain't no fool like an old fool is what they say. But least we old-timers don't have so long left to fret over the mistakes we make.'

His tone was strong and unwavering again. But there was still more than a hint of sadness in his dark eyes as he shifted his gaze between the woman and the Virginian.

'Think I'll be more inclined to give thanks for deliverance than to regret what never was,' Mary-Ann said grimly. 'Those fences must mean we're coming close to where this Attwood man is living, you think?'

'And where Mr Steele is plannin' on doin' what he can't bring himself to talk about, I think?' Amos Quinn added, his attitude toward the younger man seemingly hardening in relation to the degree of humiliation he thought he had endured as a result of the Virginian's refusal to say what he wanted to hear.

'Since you and the lady started to toss this bone between you, I haven't had much of a chance to say anything, feller,' Steele said evenly.

'Figure if you'd wanted to have a gnaw on it yourself, ain't much either of us could've done to stop you.'

'Same as anything you want to do and anybody who'd like to keep you from doing it,' the woman added, and tried to sound less bitter, and therefore less caring, than Quinn.

The Virginian wanted to counter this with a question about how he had managed to get himself caught in the trap of feeling obligated to this old man and not so old woman if he really was the kind of *mean and selfish animal* she considered him. But he suddenly felt concerned that such a query might open up a subject he preferred to stay closed.

'Whatever was or wasn't before this morning, when the trouble got started, I reckoned I owed you two,' he said, too quickly and needing to make more effort than was comfortable not to sound embarrassed. 'Reckoned, too, we were in a situation I was more familiar with than either of you.'

'Sure can't argue with the second part of that, young feller, but how come you figure a debt to — '

'You don't have to think you're sounding condescending, Mr Steele,' Mary-Ann put in, aggrieved. 'I know that *I* certainly came to trust you to protect Mr Quinn and myself as the days on the trail went by.' Then her tone and expression and even the way she turned in her saddle to glower at him were all component parts of the utter contempt she felt for him as she accused: 'Until you submitted without protest to having us all captured. Then put the lives of everyone at risk – even got that unfortunate soldier killed – in the impulsive escape — '

'Hey now, Mrs Slattery . . . Mary-Ann, my dear,' Amos Quinn cut in. 'If you'd took the time to think about what Mr Steele done all through the time since that Injun got the drop on us, you'll figure he done right by us all down the line.'

'Right?' she flared. 'Why, when I went for that grinning Indian and he had the chance — '

'Chance to get all of us shot dead is what it was, Mary-Ann!'

Quinn interrupted with the stern manner of experience chastising naïvety. 'With all them guns coverin' us. No, honey, he made his play when there was just the Injun close by. And the Injun had his mind on other things. Like Steele says, he's been in that kinda tight corner more than me. But I used to be a gunsmith. I heard enough stories from gunslingers – and witnessed enough gunfights for myself – to know when a man of that kind is doin' things right or doin' them wrong. And — '

'And what about this dying soldier?' the woman demanded. 'And the young one who was shot? Even the officer? If we had never allowed ourselves to be made hostages, maybe — '

'Maybe is the same as if, ma'am,' Steele said. 'Just isn't any point at all in looking back on what's been done and thinking anything that starts with either of those words.'

'Ah, so you can speak for yourself?' she said sardonically.

'Amos Quinn likes to talk and there's no point in me repeating what he says.'

'I cover it all, young feller?' the old-timer asked confidently, and now seemed to be taking pains to realign himself with Steele.

'Except for the other reason I decided to get clear of that way station when I did.'

'I must have overlooked thinkin' of that reason,' Quinn excused with a pensive shaking of his head.

'The talk I heard about the kind of man Cornelius Attwood is,' Steele told him, as they came around the curve of the trail in the fold of the first two fenced-off hills. All three of them saw a gleam of light in the darkness ahead.

'Guess that could be the ranch house,' Quinn growled, disconsolate again as he eyed the single point of bright yellow that had a flickering effect and sometimes appeared to go out for more than a second. Then there was nervousness in his tone as he added pointedly: 'Where we're gonna part company?'

'I'll be happy to keep travelling with you, old man,' Mary-Ann said, and there was a note of anxiety in her tone.

Steele, too, felt a disconcerting grip of concern at the pit of his stomach, which left him disinclined to wonder whether it was the uncertain future or the suddenly vaguely tense present that was worrying the others. For, as he glanced with apparent scant interest in every direction instead of concentrating his attention on the lamp-lit window that glowed or was dark in relation to the trees between it and the slow-moving trio on the trail, the Virginian was exclusively engaged in trying to find substance for the nagging doubt about the seeming emptiness of the terrain on three sides of him.

Behind was the trail across the arid desert, hidden now behind the bulk of a hill. But nobody had been close enough when the flatland was in sight to pose a threat now that there was nearby cover. Cover in the form of the hills themselves, rising irregularly up toward smooth ridges from the barbed wire fences to either side of the trail: and the rocky humps and hollows, clumps of brush and stands of timer that were sparsely featured across the broad grassy slopes of the sides of the gently arcing valley. He knew that a score or more of men could be concealed within effective rifle range of the trail, to ensure that the wagon was constantly under threat from the moment they first glimpsed the light until they were in the stand of pine and spruce out of which it gleamed. But he did not feel threatened by the watchers he could sense observing him. Who were not, he at length concluded, secreted on the flanking hills. Instead, they waited in the fringe of the trees to the right of the trail from which the light appeared to come and go. And, in fact, he saw as the gap between wagon and timber closed to a hundred and fifty yards, the two men had been hidden only by moon shadow and distance. There had been nothing furtive about the manner in which they had sat easily on a tree root, their rifles resting across their knees. Neither was there any latent menace in the way they rose, one hand fisted around the rifles which were pointed at the needle-spread ground, as their other hands were lifted to tip their hats.

'Evenin' to you, strangers,' the taller of the sheepskin-coated, Stetson-hatted, spur-booted men greeted as the team and saddle horses were reined to a halt a few feet short of where the pair of riflemen stood, their faces shadowed by the trees and the brims of their hats.

'Evening,' Mary-Ann Slattery responded, and the release of the tension that had been steadily building within her was plainly heard in the breathlessness of the single word.

'Howdy, young fellers,' Quinn added, after letting out his pent-up breath in a low whistle. 'That there the North Bend house back in these here trees?'

Steele continued to distrust the peaceful tranquillity of his surroundings, while he had to make a conscious effort not to feel like a fool playing host to seemingly groundless doubts.

'Adam Steele doesn't do much talking,' the woman explained. She was closest to the unaggressive sentries, and perhaps saw rather than merely sensed a change in their attitudes. Certainly her own manner altered – she was abruptly anxious again.

'More the man of action, maybe?' the shorter of the men on the ground suggested.

It had been a very long time since the Virginian had regarded himself as foolish for preparing to meet danger in a situation that proved to hold no threat – for too often had the sense of menace been solidly based, and his survival had depended upon his instant readiness to counter attack. Thus was he able, invariably until tonight, easily to put unfounded fears behind him with a brief awareness of relief. But now that he continued to experience a brand of threat that did not so much menace him with physical violence . . .

'Somebody should take some action on the man tied to the wagon-seat, feller,' Steele cut in on his own train of thought that was heading toward a disturbing conclusion.

'Dear God, yes, what am I thinking of,' the woman blurted. 'I don't suppose there is a physician in the immediate neighbourhood?'

'No ma'am, there ain't,' the shorter rifleman replied.

'Had a doctor stayin' on the place a couple of weeks last fall,' his partner added. 'But usually, like now, anybody gets real sick, we have to send way over to Santa Laguna thirty miles from the west boundary of the spread — '

'Well, for pity's sake, can we take this soldier to the house and see that he gets some rest in comfort?' Mary-Ann demanded, shrill anger with the unfeeling quiescence of all the men around her displacing the nervousness of two of them.

'Yeah, we oughta do somethin' for the poor young feller,' Quinn agreed, and remained disturbed by the almost eerie quality of the atmosphere where the trail ran past the timber, lit by the light that now gleamed steadily out of the darkness. And found he was unable to draw any comfort when he glanced at Steele – for the man he had come to expect to appear unshaken in every situation was now showing an uncharacteristic frown.

'It's just a little old line shack back in the woods here,' the taller guard said dolefully. 'Nothin' more than four walls and a roof, stove that ain't lit now and the lamp that is. He won't be no more comfortable in there as he is now, I'd say.'

'Sounds like they're comin', Irv,' the second sentry announced, cocking his head to the side to ask tacitly for silence.

And he got this, Mary-Ann confining her anger to a glower that she apportioned equally among the men before she found her own attention captured entirely by the rising volume of sound from around the curve of the trail beyond the timber and shoulder of the hill to the south. A body of sound composed of many shod hooves hitting hard-packed ground at a canter. Muted by distance for a few seconds, but speedily swelling in the surrounding silence of the night.

'Sonofabitch, it sounds like an army!' Amos Quinn rasped, and tore his gaze away from the point where the riders would first show.

'Guess that's pretty much what it is, stranger,' one of the guards answered absently as they both continued to peer in the direction from which the thunder of hooves came.

'And in the kinda battles Mr Attwood fights,' Irv augmented in a more forceful tone as he bleakly scanned the old-timer up on the stalled wagon, and the Virginian and the woman flanking him astride the unmoving horses, 'folks are either with him or against him.'

'Fence sitters are liable to lose what it is they're sittin' on,' his partner added.

'But this is none of our business!' Mary-Ann countered.

'Then you should've got while the gettin' was good, uh Nelson?' Irv answered, returning his attention to the southern stretch of trail, as yet still empty.

'Right, Irv.'

'Mr Steele?' the woman implored.

'Young feller?' Amos Quinn growled in the same tone of pleading.

The Virginian shifted his troubled gaze from the arrogantly imperturbable Irv and Nelson to look into the agitated faces of the skinny old-timer and sexually alluring widow woman. And for a stretched second he seemed on the point of unleashing a savage fusillade of snarling invective at them. But abruptly he seemed to be as calmly composed as the two Attwood men under the trees until, as the pounding of hooves on the hard-packed ground rose toward a crescendo, a killer's grin drew back his lips from his gritted teeth and injected a liquid glitter into his dark eyes.

'What . . . ?' the old-timer managed to squeeze out before fear of Steele constricted his vocal chords into strangled silence.

'. . . are you going to do?' Mary-Ann Slattery completed after swallowing hard just a minuscule part of the dread the Virginian had triggered within her.

'What I do best,' Steele rasped through his clenched teeth, not caring that the response was masked by the sounds of the closing riders as those at the front showed on the curve of the trail. Unconcerned, too, that the look fixed to his features and the way he continued to direct it at Quinn and Mary-Ann caused them to think that every iota of his brutal rage was aimed at them. Then he added in a whisper that was little more than a flowing of expelled breath between his teeth and through his lips that were now pursed: 'Kill people.'

'Hey, Irv!' Nelson snarled, tugging on his partner's coat-sleeve and gesturing with his unaimed rifle to draw attention to the Virginian.

But as the body of more than thirty riders, with an enclosed wagon bringing up the rear, streamed fully into sight and slowed towards a yelling, snorting, spitting, quivering and dust-billowing halt, Adam Steele's lean face and compactly-built frame eased into an expression of equanimity and an attitude of self-confident nonchalance caused Irv to do an uncomprehending double-take at Nelson, Mary-Ann and Quinn: who were all still in awe of the power for evil they had seen emanating from the Virginian.

'Say, you got to be the people that murdering crud held prisoner out at the way station in the canyon?' a man demanded from among the agitated group of newcomers, who were trying to recover their wind and calm their mounts. 'What happened up there? Goddamnit, that better not be the Italian's carcase you got strung up there on the wagon!'

The man who bellowed the stream of questions and finished with the implied threat was as angry with the men and horses hindering his eager progress from the centre toward the head of the raggedly-halted column of riders as with the strangers – who realized this had to be Cornelius Attwood.

'He's one of the soldiers from the escort detail, sir, and in a pretty bad way,' Amos Quinn hurriedly explained.

'Well, that's good,' the railroad baron announced with relief, as he plunged clear of the press.

'I doubt Sergeant Delany would agree with you, Mr Attwood,' the woman muttered acidly.

'The Italian's still at the way station?'

'Alive and well when we escaped,' Mary-Ann reported, recovered sufficiently from her recent fear to experience and project exasperation with everyone she peered at as she pleaded: 'Now please may we be allowed to do what we can for this injured man?'

'Do whatever the hell you like, ma'am,' came the disinterested response. But then Cornelius Attwood smiled with keen anticipation as he rose to a stand in his stirrups so that he was able to peer excitedly over the top of the old-timer's wagon and along the trail that led from the lush hill country and across the scrub desert to the canyon. 'I and my men are going skunk hunting!'

Irv and Nelson swung around and headed fast into the trees toward the line shack as the men who had come up the trail with Attwood now readied themselves for the next stage of the trek northward.

'Young feller?' Amos Quinn asked with disconsolate resignation

– in the manner of a man who is certain he is going to get an unfavourable reply to a request that he must nevertheless make.

'Yeah?' the Virginian said as he backed his stallion away from the wagon and wheeled him through a half turn.

'That Italian don't mean nothin' to you, way I see it?'

Mary-Ann Slattery pointedly avoided looking toward Steele, but it was obvious she was eager to hear his reply. And strained to pick up what he was saying against the raucous din of the column of men spurring their mounts forward.

'Me leaving the Count just doesn't add up so well, old man. In my book, it's not in keeping.'

ELEVEN

CORNELIUS ATTWOOD was not a big man physically, and there was nothing about him when he was not imposing his will on others that set him apart from those around him.

He was middle-aged and medium stature, with an undistinguished face given not much more character by a small moustache and a goatee that were entirely grey; while some streaks of a darker colour still showed in the thinning hair on his head. This pomaded hair was seen, shiny in the moonlight, when the unlikely-looking railroad magnate raised his hat to wave it vigorously in the air to signal a restart of the interrupted ride northward. This hat, and the rest of Attwood's attire was cut to a Western pattern but made of fabrics and fancied up with piping and fringes and buttons that advertised Eastern manufacture – and a price, maybe, that would have purchased a half-dozen genuine and far more serviceable outfits.

Some dozen or so other men who rode in the dust-stirring column that followed Attwood around the other side of the chattel-laden wagon from where Steele sat his stationary stallion, were dressed similarly in high-fashion variations of the cowpuncher's garb – or were attired in city style. Like the Virginian, but their suits and boots and shirts and cravats were more newly purchased from stores a long way to the east of El Paso, and were marked only by the dust of the short ride from the North Bend house.

Most were in the same age group as Attwood and some of them flaunted their comparable wealth with the rings on their fingers, watch chains across their bellies and stickpins in their neckwear. Some of the rich men were as fervently eager as Attwood to reach the way station in the distant canyon, while a few had to fake enthusiasm as they attempted to mask discomfort and weariness or, in one or two instances, anxious misgivings.

The majority of the riders who moved in the wake of Attwood wore the workaday garb and had the element-roughened complexions of ranch hands and cowpunchers, wranglers and farmers, or perhaps just drifters hired on. In an age group from fifteen to fifty, most of them were tall. But not all were broad – those that were had a stamp of physical strength that was totally lacking in the frames of the rich men who seemed either under-nourished or over-self-indulged. And even the eldest and skinniest of the working men – who drove the city-style tradesman's delivery wagon at the rear of the column – looked to be in better physical shape than most of his far richer contemporaries.

It took the entire body of Attwood's men just a few seconds to swing around Quinn's wagon and break into a trot along the curving trail between the fences beyond the timber. But even before the enclosed wagon – which smelled strongly of kerosene – had squeezed past the flatbed after Mary-Ann impatiently moved her mount out of the way, Adam Steele felt the warning heat of fresh self-anger. But was able immediately to smother this futile emotion, which this time was triggered by random notions of no consequence – he was simply irritated with himself for making judgments of this large group of individuals based solely on his first impressions as they rode by him in moonlight and shadow.

It was wrong to make such assessments, and he seldom did so at times when his verdict mattered. Here and now it was totally unimportant.

'If we never get to see each other again, young feller,' Amos Quinn said woefully as the Virginian heeled his horse in the wake of the trundling delivery wagon, 'want you to know I'm grateful for the help you give me back in Barclay.'

'It would be less than the truth if I said I didn't agree with Mr Quinn in that regard, Mr Steele,' the woman called stiffly after the departing rider.

This as the lighted window of the line shack in the trees was darkened. Then, a few moments later, as the sound of many hooves on the trail diminished, the more muted thud of those of two horses came from out of the timber.

'Come along, old man,' Mary-Ann urged as she moved her

mount back to its accustomed place beside the wagon. 'Let's get this poor man somewhere we can at least make him comfortable.'

Irv and the shorter Nelson emerged from the trees and swung their horses toward the north as Quinn vented a soft sound of satisfaction with a decision made.

'Something, old man?' the woman asked.

He shook his head in a conspiratorial manner, then inclined it to acknowledge the gestures of the two Attwood men, who touched their hat brims before spurring their mounts toward the Virginian who was still the back marker of the column.

'Been thinkin' that none of us thought to tell that Attwood feller or any of his men that the soldier who brought the message and the dead officer outta the canyon is one of the outlaws, Mary-Ann.' He spoke slowly, without pause for breath. Then sucked in deeply of the chill night air and used it to power a forceful spit between the rumps of the two horses in the wagon traces.

'Appears to me,' the woman answered, matching the pace of her mount to the speed of the wagon after the old-timer had set it rolling, 'that a great many questions were not asked. And so were not answered.'

'Might have bothered me some, if the young feller hadn't gone along with that bunch that's got the look of a lynch mob.'

'Me, too,' the cavalry sergeant said in a tone of voice that sighed with strain as he raised his bandaged head and straightened up from the supporting ropes.

'How long — ' Quinn started as he hauled on the reins.

'Keep moving!' Mary-Ann instructed, then moderated her tone as she peered with deep concern into the face, wan beneath the tan, below the blood-stained and sweat- and dust-sullied dressing to ask: 'Are you able to see clearly? Is the pain bearable? Should we stop for you to . . ? The Attwood house is not very far now and if you can manage to — '

'Appreciate all you people have done for me, ma'am,' the square-faced, red-haired, stockily-built sergeant cut in: after blinking his doleful eyes several times to clear his vision, and cautiously shaking his head to experiment for different levels of discomfort. 'Feel as weak as a new-born infant, and my skull hurts like . . . but far as I'm concerned, greater distance you put between me and this crazy-ass – beg pardon, ma'am – this . . . this . . . business — '

'Crazy-ass just about covers right this whole business, soldier,' Amos Quinn said. 'And I reckon Mrs Mary-Ann Slattery here ain't in no mind to take offence at a man cussin' a little?'

'I've been thinking of a few choice epithets of my own,' the woman answered absently as she looked back over her shoulder after studying Delany for long enough to be assured he was being restored to full consciousness. For stretched seconds, as Quinn drove the wagon with one hand and helped the sergeant get free of the rope restraints with the other, there was a sorrowful quality in the attitude of the widow woman, twisted in the saddle. Then, as she abruptly swung around to put her back pointedly to the three riders at the rear of the column, just before the curve in the trail took them out of sight, she seemed abruptly to be embarrassed that her innermost feelings had been displayed. And, concerned that the quizzically-gazing old-timer might voice a query she would not wish to answer, she hurried to add: 'Only ones I feel sorry for are the unfortunate Count and that young soldier.'

'That foreigner knew the risks, and Corporal Rivers ain't doin' nothin' but his duty, ma'am,' Delany told.

'Same as that Adam Steele finally figured out he had to do, seems to me,' Amos Quinn growled: as the cavalryman got free of the ropes.

'Duty? A guy like he is don't know what the word means!' Delany spoke with vicious spite, his knuckles whitening with the force of his grip on the front and side of the seat. 'That kind cares only about himself and what he can get out of — '

'That's not entirely true, Sergeant,' the woman said morosely. And Delany, who had made the denunciation and Quinn, who was about to spring to the Virginian's defence himself, both looked toward her with amazement. 'He may, indeed, care only about his own interests in untroubled times. But if he did not try to help those in need when he is called upon, he would never be able to enjoy the peace of mind that — '

'Yeah, ma'am, a man can feel real easy in his mind when he's riding' with a whole bunch of men against a handful. And the bunch is headed up by that power-crazy Cornelius Attwood who'd rather see his Pa and Ma killed than hand over a penny to a blind beggar without legs and just one arm.'

The sergeant's bitter contempt was equally shared between the Virginian and the railroad baron. While he spoke, the old-timer shook his head in tacit denial, then said in a hard tone and with a grim expression that warned against argument:

'Whatever that young feller is, he ain't yellow!'

'And I would say,' Mary-Ann added with a measured nodding of her head, 'that it was his realization at first hand of the kind of man Attwood is that made up his mind he must go back to the way station.'

Sergeant Delany remained poised to counter the assertion for a few moments as the wagon with its one escorting rider trundled through the cold, brightly moonlit night. But then he sighed and shrugged his shoulders as he raised a hand off the seat to explore the blood-crusted bandage at his temple. And then tried to let the subject be with the platitude: 'We're all entitled to our own opinions.'

'Which some of us change from time to time,' Quinn muttered, with a sidelong glance at the woman.

She met his faintly-troubled gaze with a frank one of her own. Then smiled wanly and said: 'I'm a woman and it's my privilege to change my mind. What's your excuse, old man?'

'Senility?' he suggested with an almost toothless smile of his own. 'Or right now, it could maybe be one of them cases of absence makin' the heart grow fonder, you think?'

The never firmly-fixed smile now drained out of the woman's face, gaunt with weariness. And she was melancholic for just a few moments as she looked back over her shoulder at the empty trail again. Before she expressed a grim determination that also sounded in her tone, when she abruptly faced front and replied: 'Intend to try my very hardest to make it a case of out of sight out of mind, old man.'

The man Mary-Ann Slattery was intent upon forgetting continued to ride behind the oil-tainted wagon at the rear of the column that now moved at an easy walking pace: north of the lush hill country, out on the scrub desert.

He shared this drag position with Irv and Nelson who rode alongside him to the right. There had been some low-toned talk among the three of them, all of it unconcerned with recent events and the purpose of tonight's ride. Then as easy silence descended over the trio, the two Attwood men seemingly imbued with the same kind of expectant excitement as most of the others in the unhurried column advancing toward the canyon in the distant mountain range, while Adam Steele displayed nothing of what he was thinking. Until, after a while, his lack of expression was misunderstood by Nelson, who asked with a wry grin:

'You havin' second thoughts about what you're doin' messin' in this business, Steele?'

'Seems like a lot longer ago than this morning when I had those, feller,' the Virginian answered absently.

'Uh?'

'It's more like the ninety-second that have got me back-tracking on this trail,' he explained.

'Tell you somethin' for nothin', mister,' Irv growled.

'It's all I'm willing to offer.'

'I think you're nuts. Given the choice between comin' out here to mix in with Attwood business and ridin' the other way with that fine lookin' woman for company, I wouldn't have to think twice about it.' He pursed his lips and shook his head. 'Yessir, some kinda nut is my opinion.'

Nelson eyed Steele anxiously after grimacing at his partner – like he thought Irv might have overstepped a dangerous mark with the stranger. But then he vented a muted sigh of relief when he saw the Virginian give an almost imperceptible nod of agreement, before he murmured:

'Used to be a tough one to crack. Reckon it's about time I came out of my shell.'

TWELVE

NELSON QUINCY did most of the talking in response to Steele's desultory questions, while Irving Shaw mostly did little more than offer monosyllabic agreement with his partner's contentions from time to time. Very occasionally, the less talkative man put forward an opinion of his own. But on one point, they were both firmly agreed.

Merle Thorne had good reason to carry a grudge against Cornelius Attwood, who he blamed for the deaths of his wife and baby daughter.

The tragedy had happened in the late fall of the previous year, at the height of a raging thunderstorm that had caused flash floods all over north eastern Arizona.

Thorne had been foreman of the North Bend spread then, and in the evening of the day when the grey skies had never ceased to deluge the country across hundreds of square miles with an unprecedented downpouring of torrential rain, he and Charles Smiles, who was the ranch dogsbody, and Doc Harding, who was the cook, and Attwood himself were playing cards in the big and palatial house. Attwood was losing heavily and his three workers were all winning. Rich as he was, the railroadman vacationing on his ranch hated to lose any kind of money in a card game. And invariably he never finished up losing, since his stake was always sufficient to carry him through until the cards began to run his way.

For a long time that rain-lashed night in the big ranch house, Quincy said and Shaw agreed, the three men who were winning were as eager to keep on playing as was the one who was losing. More than a handful of other North Bend men would bear witness to this, these two were anxious to assure Steele. For the bad weather had kept most of the hands close to the house; and as news of the high stakes card game was broadcast, everyone was drawn to the room where it was being played. And Thorne, who was the biggest winner – close to ten thousand dollars at one time, it was estimated by several of the watchers – was the least inclined of any of the players to call a halt to the game.

Until Luther Schuler galloped his horse in off the range to warn there was a danger of the North Bend Creek bursting its banks, up above the hollow where the foreman's house was sited. Schuler, who was unanimously disliked as the most cowardly cowpuncher on the ranch, claimed he had not been able to make himself heard by Mrs Thorne above the din of the storm. But what he did succeed in doing at the big house was to convey the urgency of the situation out at the Thorne place.

The foreman wanted to be through with the card game then. To go with whoever was prepared to ride with him out to his house and make sure his wife and baby were safe. But the rich man who employed every man in the room made an offer that caused them all to stop short as they were about to rush out into the storm-filled night.

'Merle and Attwood only. The Apache and that fat little creep of a cook could keep the couple of hundred bucks each of them had won,' Quincy told Steele in a tense tone of remembered high emotion. 'Double or nothin' for three times on hands as they were dealt. Merle had six thousand three hundred and fifty on the table in front of his chair when Attwood made the offer, Steele.'

'Ain't no man that was in that room'll ever forget that amount, I figure,' Irving Shaw said with a shake of his head in rueful reflection.

'Except for Attwood, I guess. Peanuts to him, but real important right there and then. When Merle asked Charlie Smiles to count up that money. And, while the Injun was doin' the countin', Merle kept on askin' Schuler how bad the river was. And makin' excuses about why a few more minutes wouldn't make no difference.'

'Fifty thousand and eight hundred bucks is what he stood to walk away with if he won them three hands, mister,' Shaw put in. 'I reckon that's an amount not even Cornelius Attwood's likely to forget easy?'

Nelson Quincy did not respond to the implied query. 'Not gonna make no excuses for myself or anyone else in that room, Steele,' he murmured, gazing at, but obviously not seeing, the rear of the strong-smelling wagon as the column made relentless progress across the scrub desert in the chill, brightly moon-silvered night. 'One of the men in that room had spent his life makin' a fortune and I guess just couldn't abide the thought of losin' even a little piece of it to the likes of Thorne. Rest of us couldn't do much more than hope to have us a pile of money – until somethin' like that happened. It was just too much for Merle Thorne to turn his back on. And wasn't one of us watchin' who was ready to turn our backs on what was happenin' and go out . . .'

The ranch hand shrugged his shoulders and showed an expression that revealed he knew he was trying, not for the first time, to absolve himself from what happened to the foreman's wife and child.

'Thorne won twice,' he hurried on, no longer lost in the past. 'Had twenty five thousand four hundred ridin' on the last deal. Pair of deuces lost to a pair of fives. He was cleaned out. And we all rode like bats outta hell to get to his place. Attwood as well. But the house wasn't there no more. Just part of the smoke stack was still standin'. Took two days to find his wife's body. Never did turn up the baby. They ain't very big at six months or so.'

The Virginian, as the mountains they were riding toward began to show up larger in perspective while the hills behind them got smaller, asked an infrequent question. 'His wife — '

Quincy cut in before Steele could get any further: 'She was a fine woman, but she couldn't do nothin' to help herself or their baby in a storm and flood like that one. See, she was a real bad cripple.'

'Some kinda wastin' disease,' Shaw added. 'Had to have sticks to walk with.'

'Ain't much more to tell, Steele,' Quincy took up the story again. 'Thorne buried his wife and rode on out. Along with Charlie Smiles who was his sidekick from way back when. Hardin' and Schuler, they got fired a couple of weeks later. For nothin' in particular, far as anyone knew. Just on account of, we figure, havin' them around reminded Attwood that maybe the woman and baby died because — '

'If I was Merle Thorne, reckon I'd blame him sure enough,' Shaw growled and directed a stream of saliva at the trail. 'To try to keep from blamin' myself so much. But no one'll ever know if that woman and kid'd still be alive and kickin' if we'd gone lookin' to save them fifteen minutes earlier, Nelson?'

'That's absolutely right,' Quincy said.

And both of them looked questioningly at Steele, who ignored the obvious plea for reassurance to ask:

'What happened to the soldier who hauled in the dead captain and delivered the message from Thorne, feller?'

'Laid out alongside the captain in a barn back of the North Bend ranch house, mister,' Irving Shaw answered with grim satisfaction.

'He was expected, Steele. This whole ambush and holdin' hostage business was known about from almost the time Merle Thorne first thought it up.'

Now Nelson Quincy expressed the same brand of satisfaction as his partner when they both saw the angry surprise that came and then was instantly gone from the face of the Virginian, gaunt with weariness, dirt-ingrained and heavily-bristled.

'Mr Attwood didn't know about you and that woman and the old-timer, of course,' Shaw was quick to explain. And Steele did not fail to register that the railroad baron was invested with the common courtesy title again, now that his hired hands were moving back into alignment with him, after dwelling on a part of the past that had briefly turned them against him. 'Just that Thorne and the Injun and Hardin' and Luther Schuler and a couple of men that got fired off one of his railroads back east and were in the army now were gonna jump this Italian guy somewhere out along the trail and . . .' He shrugged. 'Well, just like it happened, mister. Man that fired Ehrman and that other guy . . .'

'Greg Priest,' Quincy supplied.

'Yeah, him. Guy that fired them back east, he's stayin' at the ranch. Not by any accident, either. He's ridin' up ahead of us in this bunch now. He spotted that soldier with the dead officer right off. And just as soon as the soldier gives the message, Mr Attwood asks him right out if he's in the plot. The guy didn't say anythin'. Just started to shake his head. Which was when Mr Attwood give us the signal. And me and Nelson shot that guy dead. Plumb centre of the heart. Then we rode on out to the north pasture line shack to keep watch out for any move Merle Thorne might make that Mr Attwood didn't know about already. While him and the rest got ready to roll like we are now. About cover everythin', Nelson?'

'Reckon between us we done that, Irv,' the other man riding in the three-abreast line with the Virginian said. 'Except I think Mr Attwood would want us to warn this guy not to mess in any business that ain't his own?'

It was both a threat and a query, delivered and posed in tone and by expression.

'Reckon Cornelius Attwood and I are in the same business tonight, feller,' Steele drawled.

'Uh?' Shaw grunted.

'That's good,' Quincy said.

And the Virginian looked at them with more than just a cursory glance for the first time. Saw them as more than just two ranch hands, one a little taller than the other. Quincy was in his mid thirties, thin-faced but with a broad build. While Shaw was a few years younger and a couple of inches taller than his partner. Darker haired and complexioned, and probably women would consider him the better looking of the two.

'Somethin' botherin' you, mister?' Shaw asked, disconcerted and ready to be angry at the appraising attitude of Steele.

'Trying to quit making snap judgments about people. But I reckon we've worn down enough horseshoe and chewed enough fat for me to know that you fellers are ranch hands who do a little killing on the side – instead of the other way around?'

'Uh?'

'Seein' as how you and Mr Attwood have common interests tonight, Steele,' Quincy said in the wake of Shaw's puzzled grunt, 'I don't figure that should worry you?'

'Heading back up this trail because I have to live with my conscience. After I wasted time with the woman and the old-timer. Have to go back and get the Italian and the corporal away from there. No charge for that because it's for my own peace of mind. But if Attwood hasn't hired on professional guns to take care of the killings . . . well, I'd like to know if I'll be taking money out of your billfolds if I offer my services and he hires me to — '

Shaw vented a harsh laugh.

Quincy eyed Steele with incredulity for the duration of the truncated sound, then rasped: 'You ain't blind, so you gotta be stupid, mister? Cornelius Attwood has got himself a small army on the march here. Maybe we're all either soft-handed pen pushers or money dealers or whatever or we're hard-asses range riders. But we all got weapons we can use. Thorne and his bunch ain't no different from us, but there's a whole lot more of us than them.'

'Right!' Irving Shaw snarled, eager to contibute to the rancorous censuring of the Virginian. 'So how the hell do you figure you can make it worthwhile for Mr Cornelius Attwood to put up cash money — '

The man curtailed what he was saying and looked suddenly anxious as a rider slowed his horse until the wagon had rolled on by and then matched the pace of the trio of men behind it. The newcomer to the end of the column was the physically medium-sized, exceptionally rich railroadman whose eyes and teeth gleamed in a too-cheerful smile as he looked across the heads of the mounts of Shaw and Quincy at the Virginian, and said brightly:

'Forgive the intrusion, gentlemen. But during what has been until now a rather tedious ride, I have found it increasingly difficult to curb my curiosity about you, Mr Steele. And now I find I have timed my arrival with you at a most propitious moment. I now know you hope you get paid for being with me. Like Nelson and Irving, I am now intrigued to discover precisely what it is you have to sell me that I do not already own?'

'You're looking at it, feller.'

'That hardly answers my question, sir,' Cornelius Attwood said, the veneer of good humour peeling rapidly away. 'I see just the outer shell of a man who could well be filled with so much horseshit. You surely would not expect me, as an experienced businessman, to even contemplate making a purchase until I know exactly what merchandise is on offer?'

'I wouldn't expect to get paid on anything other than results, Mr Attwood.'

'And if you fail to deliver the goods, Mr Steele?'

'You'll have lost nothing but time. And out here in the wilderness, time isn't money?'

'As a man gets older, time can get to be more precious than money.' He shook his head, as if to physically shed the notion. 'But we have to spend time getting from here to where we're going. And if you want to show me your wares, perhaps I may be prepared to invest in your scheme.' He shifted his hardening gaze from the Virginian to the two men already on his payroll, and caught them exchanging suspicious glances. 'In business, Irving, Nelson,' he told them evenly, 'a man must examine all the options when he is intent upon making a killing. Correct, Mr Steele?'

'Yeah, feller,' the Virginian replied in the same tone. 'And sometimes it's better for a man not to get it wholesale.'

THIRTEEN

IT WAS a long time short of dawn as Adam Steele rode close enough to the way station in the canyon to smell the sweetly rancid stink of death that rose up out of the well and permeated the surrounding night air. Just how long it would be until the first dirty streaks of grey began to stretch across the star-gleaming sky he had no notion. Had felt no inclination to ask the time of the gold-watch-carrying Cornelius Attwood after they shook hands on their deal, and now continued to be utterly incurious about any side issue that did not have a direct bearing on what he planned to do..

The not-quite-full moon was high and bright enough to provide as much clear light and deep shadow as he felt he needed. And he knew as much about the way station and its occupants as he needed. And he felt good . . .

For the first time in the almost twenty-four hours since he rode into this canyon of death from the opposite direction, he experienced the gratifying satisfaction of being in control of his own destiny. And in such a state of mind he was conscious of just one nagging doubt – that this intensity of contentment might expand and explode into uncontrollable euphoria. For if he was to die in this piece of Arizona Territory that already reeked with the literal stench of death, he was determined that it should be with the clear-headed resolution that he was taking a calculated risk against which he was doing his utmost to survive. He had no desire to be blasted toward eternity from out of an insulating capsule of hysterical elation. That would be worse than getting violently killed while he was caught in the trap of relationships turned sour . . .

'Mr Steele? What in God's name is happenin' here, Mr Steele?'

The Virginian's face, heavily bristled and strained with weariness was just beginning to express a grimace of self-disgust with these unbidden thoughts of what had been and what he intended never to be again: he was riding the black stallion at an easy walk, when Corporal Rivers rasped his name and the query.

Now he reined in the horse to an unabrupt halt and drew back his lips to display a grin that failed to put warmth in his dark eyes which continued to gaze fixedly at the way station some quarter mile or so away.

'Good to know they let you live, feller,' he told the cavalry non-com who was crouched in a shallow hollow additionally protected by an arc of laboriously-stacked rocks that formed a foot-high barrier between the uniformed man and the way station. A clump of chaparral on the trail side of the hollow had kept Rivers' position secret until he opened his mouth.

'That's just what they done,' the man who showed just his blond head above the snagging brush said in the same rasping tone that mixed hope with fear. 'That Apache Injun somehow got outta the station and then got behind me where I was keepin' watch without me seein' him. Could've took me prisoner again or killed me easy as winkin'. But he just jumped on my horse and rode him back to the station, whoopin' and hollerin' and laughin' fit to bust. Then I thought I was bein' real smart and sneaky myself. But they must've seen me crawlin' all the way to this spot. Threw a whole barrage of shots at me. Since when I ain't dared to move except to take the rocks outta the bottom of the hole and build me the barricade. And with no kinda weapon I guess I couldn't — '

'Charlie Smiles did it once, I reckon he could do it again, feller?'

'What . .? Oh, get outta the place and be anyplace else around here? Yeah, I guess he could, Mr Steele. Since he got away with it the first time, I been watchin' real close. Ain't seen him, but I ain't gonna swear he's still inside. Kinda means I ain't done no good at all stayin' on picket duty here? Just give that Apache and the rest of them outlaws a little fun to help them pass the time?'

'We all make mistakes, feller,' Steele answered, and heeled his mount forward at the same leisurely pace as before. 'I'm a real expert at it.'

'You're sure enough makin' one now!' the corporal called, all hope gone from his tone now, so that his voice sounded solely of fear for the slow-riding Virginian. 'Get down here in this hole and call up that army out there!'

Steele did not acknowledge the young soldier's anxious entreaty by glance or word. He was conscious that he needed to force from his mind an instinct to warn Corporal Rivers to stay down and keep out of whatever was about to happen. For he had got the man free and clear of the canyon once already – and it was his own choice to return. Just as it was the luxury of free will that had drawn Steele himself back here. And he expected Cornelius Attwood to stick to his side of the bargain – no interference with either help or hindrance unless the Virginian's failure was seen to be inevitable.

While he narrowed the distance to the way station for the next few seconds, Steele was irritated to discover another unwanted line of thought demanding entrance to his mind that he was determined to keep uncluttered by inconsequentials. Did the scared corporal actually believe that the large force of riders who matched the unhurried progress of the civilian a mile or so behind him was made up of soldiers? Certainly it would have been an easy mistake to make in the moon-silvered night over such a distance. For in his mind's eye now, as he struggled behind the shell of imperturbability to check rising anger, he saw a vivid image of the rich men and the ranch hands as he had last seen them before he began to concentrate his unwavering gaze on the way station.

No longer did the riders move in double file on the trail with the kerosene-stinking wagon bringing up the rear of the column. Now just the wagon and the four horsemen who immediately flanked it were on the relatively smooth trail. And the rest of the men were spread out to the sides in double-ranked lines of advance. Hunched in their saddles and with rifles drawn from their boots and either canted to shoulders or with the stock bases rested on thighs, the men who were doing the will of Cornelius Attwood did create an impression of a well-drilled troop of soldiers moving inexorably forward with their supply wagon . . . or ambulance.

That they were doing what was asked of them by the powerful-through-wealth railroadman rather than under orders that had come down a military chain of command was a premise upon which Adam Steele knew he could build a whole new line of distracting doubt.

Then the time for apprehensions about the actions of others and for irritability with himself was gone. As a rifle muzzle smashed another window of the way station and then the barrel was held rock steady at aim on his chest: and he reined in his mount more sharply than he would have wished, some hundred feet short of the nearest front corner of the building.

'Well, look who came on all the way back to see us?' the short and fat Doc Harding called in a taunting tone – sounding too far off to be the man with the rifle at the smashed window in the side wall of the place. 'He must've liked our company so — '

'Make less with the mouth, Doc!' Merle Thorne snapped. And despite the tremor in his voice, the Winchester he pointed out through the window remained totally immobile.

For the first time since riding away from the place, Steele was uncomfortably aware of the cut and dull aches in his legs from the plunge through another rifle-shattered window.

'You must be insane, *signore*!' Count Paulo Zucconi cried in a strangled tone of incredulity. 'Did not Attwood tell you — '

'The boss said to shut up, white eyes!' the Apache cut in tensely. 'Told it to Doc but meant it for all of us, I think.'

'Right, Charlie,' Thorne confirmed. 'Only man I want to hear talking for awhile is the dude.'

'And you better not move anythin' except your mouth!' Luther Schuler snarled, giving his threat emphasis by pushing his rifle into view on the other side of the shard-lined frame from where the top man's Winchester was angled.

'I've come to get Zucconi out of there, feller,' the Virginian said evenly, and complied with the order of the man with the pock-marked face: hardly moved his lips to speak the words as he continued to sit easy in the saddle, booted feet in the stirrups and gloved hands draped over the horn with the reins held between the palm of one and the back of the other.

'Easier said than done, dude,' Thorne growled. 'Not like me and Luther here – and Frank Ehrman . . .' A third rifle was pushed into sight midway between the other two and the moonlight glinted on all three barrels but did not penetrate in through the broken window to reveal the men who aimed them. '. . . blasting holes in you.'

'And you know we don't give a shit who we kill, mister!' Schuler snarled. 'Saw you and that crazy corporal chewin' the fat out down the trail there. Well, he only got to stay alive because the Injun's crazy as he is and wanted to play friggin' games with — '

'Playtime's over, dude!' Thorne cut in impatiently. 'You wanna give me the message Attwood never paid you enough to bring me?'

'Greg was supposed to bring the money, Merle . . . ask him where Greg is, Merle,' the scared-sounding trooper pleaded.

Steele felt good again. Satisfied with the knowledge that all the men were in the room behind the broken window. And of the three members of the gang most likely to be panicked into ill-timed action by the unexpected, two were at the window – so that he was their prime target. And he was master of his own fate, the outcome of which depended upon whether he had correctly assessed the kind of men he was up against, and if he was to be allowed that modicum of good luck that can turn any situation on its head.

'Because you sure as hell ain't brought the money I want in exchange for the Zucconi guy's neck,' Thorne went on, as if Ehrman had never made the tremulous interruption. 'On account of just one man was supposed to bring that fifty thousand eight hundred bucks I'm due, dude. Not one man backed by thirty-seven more.'

'And it was supposed to be Greg Priest, mister!' Ehrman complained shrilly, his rifle wavering from side to side and up and down. 'If that bastard Attwood's done for my buddy, I'll swear I'll — '

'It's my intention to get the Count out of there for about a tenth of that, feller,' Steele drawled. 'A round five thousand.'

'You die cheap, mister!' Luther Schuler snarled.

The Virginian murmured: 'Who the hell wants to be one of the dear departed?'

FOURTEEN

HE BEGAN to voice the low-toned sardonic comment while he still appeared to be sitting in a nonchalant attitude astride the unmoving stallion. And completed it as he swung violently out of the saddle while the horse, snorting at being so suddenly abused, was at the top of a harshly-induced rear.

Two rifle shots exploded in almost perfect unison and Steele was momentarily blinded by the double muzzle flashes. When he found himself peering involuntarily at the way station window because of the direction in which the horse reared and the way he twisted clear of the saddle and plunged to the ground – flinging aside the reins and sliding the Colt Hartford smoothly from the boot as he jerked his feet out of the stirrups.

Then a third shot from the darkness of the broken window sounded just the merest part of a second ahead of the crack of a bullet leaving a chamber of his own rifle. His eyes were squeezed closed now: not to guard against another instant of blindness from dazzle as such – rather as part of a reaction to the fierce bolt of pain that hit him as he crashed to the hard-packed dirt. He also gritted his teeth and rasped a profanity through them. And in the next instant was shocked into silence by the dread thought he hurt so badly that maybe he had taken a bullet. Or two!

But, as the flailing forehooves of his horse thudded down close to where he was sprawled, he forced himself to ignore anything that he did not know for certain. Had to endure the gruelling punishment of pain, but fought to the limit of his tenacious will to survive to rise above it.

No more than three seconds had passed since the first two shots were triggered out of the way station in response to his sudden pre-emptive move. Fired by Ehrman and Schuler, he guessed.

Then he and Thorne had exchanged shots a second later. All of this in panic, anger or for effect. With nobody inclined to take the time to take aim. But in the surrounding silence that came to the canyon after the final echo of the gunfire faded from between its rock walls, Steele sensed in the way the lever actions of the three Winchesters were pumped that ice-cold determination to kill him would slow and steady the aim of the men for the next fusillade.

It took less time to thumb back the hammer of his Colt Hartford, though. And his grimace became a grin as he squeezed his trigger a second time – fired from the hip while he rose up to his knees.

'God, no!' Frank Ehrman shrieked as he staggered back from the window, withdrawing his half-cocked rifle from sight.

Steele would have preferred to gun down Merle Thorne first, but there was not yet time to select targets. He hurled himself sideways as he thumbed back the hammer again. Felt wetness on many areas of his body, but pain only from those points which twice had taken the brunt of impact from the premeditated plunges to the ground. So the moisture was sweat-oozed from tension-opened pores. No blood – yet.

Two more shots exploded through the moonlit night: to add their acrid taint of black powder smoke to that which already assaulted the nostrils and masked the odour of old death.

Now Steele felt his thick topcoat snagged by at least one bullet. And his grin broadened as he rolled on to his belly and came up onto all fours. Heard the beat of hooves recede as his stallion galloped up the slope of the trail toward the narrow point of the canyon. He triggered a third shot and his hat scaled off his head, torn free by a bullet from a rifle not seen at the window.

The Virginian's mouthline continued to express high humour, rooted in the sheer pleasure of survival against the odds and the knowledge that he was making this stand of his own free will on his own account. But between the gleaming whiteness of his teeth and the less stark coloration of his hair, his coal-black eyes were no longer shadowed by his hat brim: and they were seen to show a strangely contrasting expression of grim consternation as he powered to his full height.

Another rifle was gone from the window. Had slipped from the hands of the second man to take a bullet from the Colt Hartford. Merle Thorne, this time, Steele thought. If there had been no switching of positions inside the room while he had been briefly blinded or was momentarily distracted by his struggle to get up off the ground and lunge into a run: to offer himself as a constantly-moving target and then to attain cover.

Another shot was sent at him as he raced over the already trodden-down vegetables between the well and the way station. More sweat oozed from his every pore, but he felt no stunning thud – until his haste to get out of the line of fire took precedence over every other factor and he was stopped by the side wall of the way station. And was unable to check a groan of pain as his leading shoulder cracked against the stone and he bounced to the ground this time.

This fresh pain would perhaps have been insignificant had it not been the latest of many assaults on his punished frame, but as such it acted to temporarily paralyse him and deaden his senses to everything except the agony. And it seemed that each passing second was stretched to an extent that slowed every movement taking place around him – decelerated the actions and also muted the sounds of them.

He saw the wagon and the double lines of men on either side of it start toward him. And he saw Corporal Rivers rise up out of the hollow behind the protective wall of stones. He saw the length of his own body spread out in the angle of the way station wall and the ground. He saw the smashed window from a much narrower angle than before. And a single rifle barrel abruptly appeared – to be pushed out far enough for the hand that was fisted around it in front of the frame to be seen.

A man said: 'You two-faced sonofabitch!'

It was not the man who was aiming a Winchester out of the window. Steele was unable to recognize the voice that made the contemptuous accusation. Nor was he able to move any part of his body below the neck: and felt the near euphoria that had gripped him earlier drain away from him. But something close to a smile was born out of the mindless grin that faded from his face. And he experienced a pleasing brand of quiet contentment as he waited for the rifle to swing around and aim at him.

Then two gunshots punctuated the angry words. And a man groaned in bitter disappointment rather than with pain.

Not the man at the window, though. And his rifle bucked and spat a bullet through the muzzle flash. Not at Adam Steele, who found his senses returned to normal and his muscles responding to his demands on them as the echo of this latest shot sounded off the flanking rock walls.

'I got that crazy corporal, Merle!' Doc Harding shrieked in high excitement, his rifle jerking and swaying as he eagerly pumped the lever action.

Steele snapped up into a sitting position as the fat little lip-licker vented his triumph. And as he did so, a gloved thumb easing back the Colt Hartford's hammer, the Virginian spared another glance along the moon-whitened floor of the canyon's southern length. Saw with total dispassion that the cavalryman was slumped belly upwards over his carefully constructed wall: then noted with a sudden frown of curiosity that the wagon at the very centre of the advancing lines of riders was shining with something brighter than reflected moonlight.

'Frig him, he ain't no danger to us, you crazy bastard!' Merle Thorne yelled. 'It's that damn dude we gotta — '

'Merle, the Attwood men are startin' to — ' Harding cut in, his terror out-yelling Thorne's fury.

This as Adam Steele's initial dissatisfaction that he had failed to trigger a bullet into the top man among the outlaws was displaced by anger – the change caused by the same prospect that was terrifying Doc Harding. Cornelius Attwood had ordered his small army of ranch hands and men of commerce to attack. And from a point some half mile down the canyon the wagon team was spurted from a leisurely walk into a sudden gallop: the horses urged to reach full speed and to maintain it by the crack of the driver's whip, his raucous voice and their animal instinct to run from flames and smoke. But horsesense has its limitations and the bolting geldings were unaware that the fire was raging on the wagon they were hauling. The tongues of flames licking high within moments of the firing match being lit, while the blackness and density of the smoke that trailed and spread behind the racing rig provided further evidence that it had not been an accidental spillage of kerosene that had caused the wagon to smell so strongly of oil.

Across the sparsely-featured rough ground to either side of the trail, riders raced their mounts into and out of the rolling billows of smoke, the horses perhaps dictating the pace out of panicked reaction to the stink of fire in their flared nostrils while the men in the saddles could only struggle to control the direction of the headlong gallop. This while, behind the frontrunners, the larger part of the attacking force stayed clear of the thickest clouds of rolling and twisting smoke in straggled lines and scattered groups. Some of the less skilled horseback riders were certainly forced to hold back because their mounts were unwilling to get closer to the fire. Others, though, only made a pretence of not being able to control the nervous animals: were themselves much more afraid of what lay ahead beyond the ever-moving veil of smoke.

Voices, raised to a fever pitch of excitement as men urged their mounts and themselves and those about them to finish what was started, sounded in vigorous competition with the thunder of hooves and the rattle of wheels. And over such a distance the cacophony drowned out the crackle and roar of the fire that by the moment took a hungrier, firmer, more vociferous grip on the speeding wagon.

No gunshots were triggered from the readied rifles of the horsemen: and because of this the crack of one report from close by sounded disproportionately loud to the ears of the Virginian. Who, a moment after wrenching his gaze away from the attackers, was poised to fire his own gun – remained seated on the ground with one shoulder pressed to the wall of the way station and had the stock of the Colt Hartford nestled tightly against the other one. Waiting for the grey face with its tiny red-rimmed eyes to show nervously in the narrow angle of the window as the fat little man sought sight of him.

But the revolving rifle remained unfired as Doc Harding appeared at the window – the one-time cook on the North Bend

Ranch sent forcefully forward. Until his legs came up hard against the wall beneath the window and he was whiplashed from the waist over the sill. His rifle was hurled involuntarily out on to the vegetable patch as he folded double, unfeeling hands slapping against the outside of the wall. The moonlight shone dully on the crimson slickness that oozed up out of the sparse grey hair at the nape of his neck and top of his head.

'How much?' Merle Thorne demanded shrilly. 'How much he pay you?'

Steele needed the support of the wall and of his rifle-become-a-crutch to haul himself up to his feet. The pains that streaked through his battered body, the anger he felt for Cornelius Attwood and his sense of satisfaction that – except for the rich man's unwanted intervention – almost everything had gone according to his plan, all contributed to the look of anguish that contorted the exhaustion-hung face of the Virginian.

'More than you ever could, *boss*!' the Apache roared, spitting out the final word in the venomous tone of an obscenity.

Charlie Smiles had blasted the killing bullet at Harding from low down. Steele could tell this from the trajectory the shot had followed to explode clear out of the crown of the little man's head. The Indian was on the floor of the room, he decided. Probably hurt after the exchange of shots between himself and man he had betrayed. Probably unable to see out through the window over the ledge of which Harding was slumped. So unaware of the new danger and anxiously mystified by Thorne's boast:

'Not for long, Charlie! Looks like you're about to get fired!'

He laughed. Against this nearby sound and the rising volume that came with Attwood's charging men, two pairs of footfalls slapped on the floor of the room. Then a door was wrenched open and slammed closed.

'Attwood, you sonofa . . .' Thorne began to bellow.

But a fusillade of rifle shots cracked out of the smoke to curtail or mask his words. As Steele forced himself to look away from the window with the corpse slumped through it: and was in time to see, where the smoke allowed, riders bring their sweating mounts to slithering and rearing halts. While the wagon with the skinny old-timer up on the seat kept on jolting and swaying along the trail with no slackening of pace. The driver making no attempt to control the team. Until they were about to race across the front of the way station, when he wrenched on the reins to demand a sudden turn to the right – away from the building, but the speed and abruptness of the change of course designed to tip the wagon sideways and send it slithering toward the corner of the way station. Forty feet from where Steele was pressed to the wall close to the rear corner. A lot nearer to where Charlie Smiles was frantically struggling to claw and clamber over the unfeeling form of Harding – the Apache's desperate attempts to get clear of the building hampered by the weakening bullet-wound that had blossomed blood over a wide area of his shirt front. His eyes beneath the headband with the single eagle feather in it expressed a plea for both help and understanding as he raked his gaze away from the doom-laden blazing wagon to stare at the stone-faced and unmoving Steele.

'You left it too late,' the Virginian mouthed rather than said to the Apache, who was not going to die laughing; knowing it would be impossible for him to make himself heard above the cacophony of sound as the wagon smashed into the corner of the way station with an explosive crash of splintering timber, roaring flames and screaming horses that acted to diminish the crackle of gunfire that counterpointed it.

Just for a second, before the disintegrating wagon hurled globules of flaming oil and pieces of burning debris at and between the two men, the Indian expressed something close to apology – or was it despair? – while Steele hoped he managed to convey some brand of rueful understanding. This before he saw the living and the dead men at the window engulfed in a sheath of flames: as the fire seemed to roar with greater vigour now that it had human flesh on which to feed.

Only for part of another second was the Virginian able to look at the fiery scene, before blazing debris and furnace heat forced him to demand fast movement from his punished body. Even so, as he picked himself up off the ground after swinging backwards around the rear corner and climbing up the corral fence, he had to beat at several smoking and smouldering areas of his sheepskin coat. It took him many frenzied moments to put out these potential fires. And in this time the major blaze took firmer hold on the way station, spreading across the timber roof and making inexorable progress through the room where the bodies of Ehrman and Schuler would spasm and twitch as if the men were still alive during the first few moments of the roasting.

Most of the kerosene had been burned now so that the smoke was not so black. And it spiralled vertically into the night sky now that the consuming flames were no longer streaming from the racing wagon. So, beyond the immediate area of the blazing way station, the southern length of the canyon was plainly visible again – in the moonlight and more brightly lit, close to, by the flames.

The charge had come to an end as the wagon deliberately crashed into the building, and some of the men had found it better to swing down from their saddles to calm their fire-scared mounts. Almost all the rifles, none of which had fired a shot anywhere but up at the star-gleaming sky, were back in boots. Those that were not were in the hands of the more skilled horsemen, canted to shoulders or resting on thighs as the riders urged their apprehensive mounts slowly forward. The men who needed both hands to quieten and keep calm their horses, at length rode or walked from their scattered positions toward a point on the trail where the rifle-toting half dozen had gathered in a close-knit group around Cornelius Attwood.

Nelson Quincy and Irving Shaw were among the first to move in close to the rich man, and the other four were also ranch hands, Steele saw. Then, rapidly, as if nobody – Westerner or Easterner – wanted to be suspected of holding back now that the enemy had been vanquished, the whole bunch from the North Bend spread came together again. Except for the skinny old man who had so skilfully timed the sudden turn of the team horses to send the wagon into its shattering sideswipe at the way station. He lay sprawled on the far side of the trail a little way short of the burning building, and in the flickering fringe glow of the flames. His head was set at such an angle to his body that it was obvious his scrawny neck had been snapped when he leapt to the ground from the crashing wagon.

His team were now up at the top of the rise where the canyon walls came closest together, still harnessed together and with the broken traces dragging behind them. Steele saw, too, with a grunt of satisfaction, that his own stallion had ended its bolt up there on the narrow ridge. All three horses could be seen from the far side of the corral, where the Virginian had gone at a limping run after he swung away from watching the North Bend men regroup. With the roar and crackle of flames for cover, he had no need to move stealthily across the corral between the rear of the building and the stable. The way station, not yet burning in this area, cast deep moon-shadow over him as he climbed the fence and pressed himself tight to this wall in much the same manner as when he was preparing to kill Doc Harding on the other side.

He glimpsed the horses at the top of the hill as he raked his dark-eyed gaze over the moon-bright terrain beyond the shadows: and curtailed the low venting of mild pleasure as he located Merle Thorne and Paulo Zucconi – the younger, shorter, more muscular man standing close behind his captive. Who he was holding by the collar of his suit jacket with his left hand, while his right was fisted around the butt of his Army Colt: the muzzle pressed hard against the side of the Italian's neck. Zucconi's hands were tied at the wrists behind his back. Both men were hatless.

The hostage expressed gulping terror of death as he stared directly ahead – across the front of the blazing building toward the gathering crowd of North Bend men. The captor wore a scowl of unwavering determination as he peered through narrowed eyes over the revolver in his rock-steady grip, seeing the same scene as Zucconi.

They were on the far side of the trail, lit by the flames of the fire that was raging with increasing intensity through the way station: but far enough away to be beyond the reach of the heat.

As Steele began to inch with cautious side-steps along the wall, he again became uncomfortably aware of pain. But the grimace he spread across his face was also caused by the stink from his charred coat reaching up into his flared nostrils. But even more so, he allowed, by the stomach-churning tension of knowing that a wrong move by himself or any of the many men from the North Bend spread could cause the rigidly-standing Thorne to move his index finger just the fraction necessary to blast a bullet into the head of Count Paulo Zucconi. Which would mean the Virginian could not claim the five thousand Cornelius Attwood had offered for the Italian's safe release. And, more importantly to Steele, he would have failed in the purpose he had set out to attain at a time when he had no thought of financial reward – the strange, for him, consideration that he would have to live the rest of his life with a man's death on his conscience.

'You just have to be the meanest, most black-hearted sonofabitch that ever drew breath on this earth, Attwood!' Merle Thorne blurted suddenly. He displayed no effort at raising his voice and there was no strain in his tone. But the words rang out clearly against the sounds of the fire that at once seemed muted to Steele – until he realized as he halted some ten feet short of the corner that the thud of many slow-moving hooves had previously been contributing to the body of the noise. And that the horses had been reined in as soon as Thorne began to voice his accusation.

'I ever claim to be anything else, Merle?' Cornelius Attwood countered evenly, and the Virginian judged him to be no more than fifty or sixty feet away, he and his men hidden beyond the corner of the burning building. 'You worked for me a long time and if you didn't find out what kind of man I am — '

'Yeah, I was a stupid fool!' Thorne cut in. 'Let myself get blinded to a whole lot of things because of your money. But now I've seen that nobody ever gets more than the handful of loose change you pay in wages. The big money you only use as bait to get men to do crazy stupid things for you.'

'Charlie Smiles came to me, Merle,' Attwood said, retaining his outward calm as the other man showed signs of rising emotion. And as the Virginian's grimace became a frown. 'He named the price he was asking to sell you out.'

'As much as the fifty grand I risked the lives of my wife and daughter for?' Thorne countered after using the time Attwood was talking to get a firm grip on his temper again.

Steele knew something was wrong about the stand-off out there across the trail from the burning building. Almost from the first moment he discovered that the Thorne bunch had a double crosser amongst them he had earmarked the Apache as the most likely turncoat. For the Indian had been the only member of the group who had actively avoided killing anyone. From the time when he had first got the drop on the unwelcome strangers up at the canyon narrows. And he had finally shown himself in the same light by convincing the rest they should play a scaredy-cat game with Rivers instead of killing the young cavalry corporal – before he tipped his hand and Thorne saw him backshoot Doc Harding. The Virginian had counted on the Indian making his move earlier, but . . . what he had not counted on was another Attwood ploy to ensure his former ranch foreman did not extort any money out of him.

'Nowhere near, Merle. He was just a stupid Indian. No ambition. One thousand dollars was the price of his betrayal. Offered old Ethan Lennox just half that to run the burning wagon at the way station. Figured those that were still alive inside would see him coming and have plenty of time to get out. But it seems the Apache was in no shape —'

'I shot the lousy sonofabitch when he killed Doc and before he could — '

'Way it goes, Merle. And old Ethan Lennox didn't get off the wagon the way he had planned. Broke his neck, looks like.'

'Money goes to money, not to dead men, uh Attwood?'

'That surely is right, Merle. So — '

'The dude that could've killed Charlie when he busted himself and his friends and the soldiers out of here? Another one got killed himself from trying to earn a whole bundle of Attwood dollars?'

'He came high, Merle. Five thousand was what he wanted. Seems he's some kind of drifting gunslinger looking for a place to settle and start raising high-class horseflesh. I started from nothing myself, Merle. You know that from when you worked for me. And I admire men of ambition and enterprise. Gave him a good chance to earn the money he wanted in the way he wanted: so that he wouldn't have that man's death on his conscience, giving him restless nights when he finally got his stud.'

The fire had reached into the room beyond the wall against which Adam Steele was pressing his back. The stones started to feel warm even through the thickness of his coat, and then he began to hear them as they fed on fresh fuel. Or did he imagine this – a conjured-up image born out of the fire of anger that blazed and crackled deep inside him?

'. . . *that man's death* . . .' That man who was supposed to be an influential foreign envoy and good friend of Cornelius Attwood, yet to whom the railroad baron had not uttered a word of greeting or reassurance since this exchange began. That man who sounded more like a New Englander than an Italian. That man who had been able to disguise his anxiety so well for so long. But who now as he listened to the catalogue of lethal misfortune that befell men who performed special services for Attwood sank deeper into the slough of abject terror.

'Didn't give Ethan Lennox the sign to start the fire until I saw Steele go down after you and your henchmen fired on him, Merle,' the arrogant rich man, surrounded by his private army, continued in a tone that sounded of boredom in the making. 'Just as I am in no manner responsible for the Apache and Old Ethan . . . well, Merle, I guess you don't give one half of a good goddamn about my conscience being as clear as that down-on-his-luck dude gunslinger wanted his to be? So I'll tell you now that if you'll just step aside and toss away that gun, I promise you a fair trial by due process of law. Make you that promise in front of all these men here. Who don't all work for me, Merle. Good few are people I have business dealings with. And they know I don't welsh on a deal. If I did here and now, it wouldn't serve my interests well in the future.'

'While I got your friend the Count — '

But he didn't, of course. Adam Steele knew that if he had been thinking clearly from when he learned about Attwood's pre-knowledge of the ambush plot, he would have realized the life of an important foreign dignitary would not have been risked. But he had been so all-fired intent on the abstract morals of his own part in the crazy business to look for the glaringly obvious realities. *That man* was a phony. A hired substitute in a rich man's game to do unto your enemy before he does it to you – with little or no concern for the men on your side. Including the US Cavalry. But with utter certainty of which side was going to win.

The Virginian made the conscious effort to wipe the grimace of hatred off his exhaustion-lined face. His mind was drained of every last part of all thought without him needing to become aware of what was happening. And he felt not a twinge of discomfort from any area of his punished body as he swung fluidly away from the wall, brought the Colt Hartford up to his shoulder, thumbed back the hammer and squeezed the trigger.

Muzzle smoke masked his view for an instant. But then it was gone and he saw the hole in the side of Merle Thorne's hatless head, just above the man's right ear. Cold-bloodedly elected to make it a head shot in order to kill the unsuspecting man instantly and give him no time to voluntarily squeeze the trigger of his revolver. At the moment of death, a jerking nerve might have . . . but it didn't. The man whose plot it had been to get what he considered his dues from Cornelius Attwood fell sideways like a sawn-down tree, hands flopping to his sides and the right one letting go of the Colt as his head inscribed the same arc as the spray of blood and gore that came out of the bullet's exit wound.

As the dead man smacked against the ground and his former hostage sank down on to his haunches, awkwardly because of having his wrists bound firmly at his back, Adam Steele stepped into view at the corner of the blazing building. And drew the stunned gaze of everyone toward him as the first grey fingertips of approaching day took a tentative grip on the sky above the eastern rim of the canyon.

'I got a little singed, but I didn't get burned, feller,' the Virginian drawled as he canted the Colt Hartford to his left shoulder and brushed at his charred coat front with his gloved right hand.

Perhaps others in the group recovered as fast or even faster than Cornelius Attwood from the shock of one man's sudden death and the apparent resurrection of another. Steele could not tell, since he looked only at the quick-to-calm rich man whose wealth had caused so much carnage.

'As I told Thorne, sir, I never welsh on a deal,' the railroad baron said without a tremor in his voice, nor any definable expression on his neatly-bearded face. 'I brought here sufficient funds to meet the ransom demand if it had been unavoidable, so I am able to pay you right now. But perhaps you may be interested to know that you are not the only hired hand to benefit from Merle Thorne's monstrous plot to extort money from — '

The man who was not Count Paul Zucconi struggled upright and began to babble: 'I must thank you, mister. I hope you won't be mad to find out I work for one of Mr Attwood's companies back East and — '

Steele had been massaging his bare head and glancing up at the narrow point of the canyon while he needed to make a conscious effort to deny to himself that it was the aroma of roasted meat in the air that made him feel suddenly hungry. Now he cut in on the weak-with-relief man who had interrupted the one taking a bulging burlap sack out of a saddlebag. 'Just need to find my hat and get my horse. And if I'm to be paid the five thousand I'm owed here and now, I reckon . . .

. . . THERE'S NOTHING MORE TO BE SAID.'*

**But the Virginian will not be a silent partner in the third Edge Meets Adam Steele book DOUBLE ACTION, published by New English Library.*